KNOWING WONDER

Knowing Wonder

AN ELEPHANT STORY

MERRILL SAPP

Illustrations by **GARETH HOOK**

REVERBERATIONS BOOKS

For the elephants and the people

Published by Reverberations Books
Santa Cruz, California
www.reverberationsbooks.com
An imprint of Chin Music Press
Seattle, Washington
www.chinmusicpress.com

FIRST EDITION
Printed in Canada

ISBN: 978-1-63405-069-2
Library of Congress Control Number: 2024937841

Contents

Preface

The sounds of an elephant around my tent in the dark are the sounds of everything in her path yielding to her presence. Grass swishes aside for the 8,000-pound body. Leaves rustle as she forages in the trees. Otherwise, she steps silently through the night. These sounds would not have woken me. I was already listening to the lions calling a few miles away. They are relaxed, and in their element, the dead of night. The air is still, and I try to gather their voices with my ears, actively searching, wishing I could pull in the sound like scent. I have come to love the noises of animals as much as I love seeing them.

Though I have always felt a kinship with nonhuman animals, it took a fascination with those in faraway places for me to develop a reverence for the familiar in my own backyard. Now I recognize the beauty of the squirrel, busily preparing a nest for the arrival of his hairless little infants. Or the rabbits and their nervous, territorial posturing. When the female is ready to mate, she boxes the male about the face. I ponder this technique. Sometimes I sit outside at night and hope to hear the soft call of the owl whom I sometimes see at dusk. Her hoot sounds like magic but is real and right there.

When we start to see animals as they really are, or at least appreciate each animal's unique, mysterious, unknowable self, the mental boundaries we have constructed for *being human* versus *being animal* fall away. We realize each of these animals has a life of her own, and they are busy getting on with those lives all around us whether we acknowledge them or not. And when we understand that every animal is connected to something beyond, linked by ecology to living things around the earth, we know that we are all in this together.

Traveling in parts of the world where development is less pervasive than in the United States, I have been struck by the closeness of people to the reality of climate change. They are connected with the natural world and dependent on it in ways that most people in the US are not. Perhaps we notice that the weather is hotter than usual as we walk from our cars into our offices. Some are hesitant to talk openly about it, considering it a divisive political issue. I have found no such reticence in other parts of the world, where people can give personal accounts of how climate change is affecting their lives. A farmer in Kenya, a conservation leader in Sri Lanka, a wildlife specialist in Zambia—they can each describe changing weather patterns and unpredictable rains. They can explain how these changes are altering their existence, invariably making life more difficult.

Talking about nature as something separate and apart from ourselves is evidence that we feel disconnected from our nonhuman kin and the places they live. Nature is a place we visit. Meanwhile, as a society we have grown distant not only from other living beings but also the consequences of our actions. We celebrate seeing wildlife and simultaneously live in ways that daily threaten the existence of that same wildlife.

This book is a story about elephants. It is fiction, but it is not made up. The elephants in these pages are real and based on scholarly research, videos of wild animals, news reports, interviews, tales of people who live near elephants, and personal experience. The story is built on all of that.

James Raffan, author of *Ice Walker*, coined the term, "nonfictional storytelling" to describe the genre-defying mixture of science and narrative. I still don't have a good category for this book. But I know that only by knowing animals for who they are, their emotional selves, and the way they experience the world, can we comprehend the true impact of our actions—what their lives are like as the result of how we live. We would not claim to understand the lives of other people by counting them, knowing where their homes are, their method of travel, or what they eat. Animals think and learn. They have personalities and make decisions. They respond meaningfully to changes in conditions, such as predators, access to water, and the needs of their young.

Elephants are individuals who are part of a community of species who depend on each other—including humans, the only members of the community who knowingly and actively destroy the habitat that is our home. Paul Kingsnorth wrote of "the environment"—the air, the waters, the creatures, and us—that "We are it; we are in it and of it, we make it and live it, we are fruit and soil and tree, and the things done to the roots and the leaves come back to us." We are it, and it is us. And we should act as if life depends on it.

1. *In the Valley*

OCTOBER

Moyo walks in her mother's shade as they move toward the sun rising quickly in the east. Her whole body fits easily underneath Lua's big frame. Today has started like many others; in the light of early morning Moyo's family began its relaxed parade from the edge of the forest into the grass of the open savanna—the land from which they get their English moniker, savanna elephants. They are the largest and grandest animals on land.

These last few weeks have been a good time to be a tiny, 250-pound elephant, born only a month prior. It's near the end of the dry season, and Moyo's family has been staying close to the river. She's had a chance to find her feet before the rains come and her family goes on the move in search of fresh water and food. Right now, she doesn't struggle to keep up, and her only job is to drink milk and get stronger. That, and learn how to use her useless little trunk, the feature that defines an elephant more than any other. The trunk starts like a bouncy toy and becomes the most functionally complex organ of any animal. For now, she drinks by dunking her face in the water as she crouches her little body down at the edge of the riverbank.

The heat drags on with temperatures over 100 degrees, and the air is crackling with dryness. This is the hottest part of the year before the rains break in late November or December. Lua looks like an animal who lives under an unrelenting sun and a vast, open sky. Her skin has deep crevices that mimic parched earth. As family leader, Lua knows this land and where to find pools that are usually reliable for a drink, but as the hot, dry season lingers on, the water has dried up, and the plants have little to offer. It's increasingly difficult to stay close to both water and food.

After their morning forage, Lua guides her family to the bare riverbed where she hopes to find water even in the driest conditions. The elephants are listless and need more water today, especially Moyo who does not have much reserve. Lua and her companion, Sumina, slowly walk the sandy area and search for underground water. They function as divining rods, finding the precise spots that water is high enough for them to reach. Only elephants know exactly how they locate these fleeting reservoirs. They can smell water, at least at short distances, and might also feel echoes of their own footfalls with their feet through the ground above an aquifer. When Lua finds the right spot, she starts digging with her front foot, carefully moving sand. As it gets deeper, she uses her trunk to scoop and carve a narrow, cylindrical hole down into the earth.

When Lua reaches water, the hole becomes a well. After she and Sumina drink, Sumina monitors the younger elephants as they each take a turn, making sure they step gingerly around the hole and do not collapse the sides of the well. Moyo is far too little to drink here, but Lua has already shared the water directly into her mouth.

When the family has had enough to drink, Lua rumbles that it's time to leave, and they move together toward the west. After they have gone, other animals will get a much-needed drink from the elephant wells, sometimes the only available water in an area. Especially during the dry season, other animals go where the elephants go. Wildlife of all kinds, cats—both big and small—, hyenas and porcupines, impalas and warthogs, and a great variety of birds use the wells. Even local baboons serve their purpose, with little arms that can reach into the narrow holes and hand-pack the sides, helping the wells stay intact.

THE EARTH BENEATH THE FEET of these elephants is a mere shell on top of the planet. The geography of the Great Rift Valley makes this clear. Though the name Great Rift is a misnomer, an old term for what we now know to be a series of trenches that are contiguous all the way from Southern Africa to Asia, the term appropriately conveys the meaning of a long expanse of land that is shifting and being pulled apart from underneath. Water settles in these trenches, forming some of the deepest lakes in the world. The southern end of the Great Rift forms the edge of the Nyasa-Tanganyika Plateau, a spine of land that stretches across the northern part of Southern Africa.

Lua's family are elephants of the Luangwa Valley of eastern Zambia, a place sometimes described as the honeypot of Zambia for its relative lushness. The valley runs north to south in eastern Zambia. This geologically active area has fault lines that pushed up the earth around it and formed a basin in the center more than 500 miles long. Because animals don't recognize man's political borders, Lua could also be an elephant of Malawi or Mozambique, though the geographic boundary of the Luangwa River forms the main edge of her home range. Her life,

and the lives of her ancestors for the last few millions of years, has been spent trekking across this valley.

Zambia is a country of great rivers which have carved hills and valleys as they rush down from the high plateaus. The annual floods alternate with the dry season and bring life to this area neighboring the deserts of Angola and Namibia. The most famous river is the mighty Zambezi, the river of Victoria Falls, one of the Seven Natural Wonders of the World. The watershed of the upper Zambezi River runs east-west along a ridge that separates the area geographically from the drainage basin of the Congo. The Zambezi flows in a great loop that rims the bowl formed by mountains and plateaus in this part of central Southern Africa. The partial circle of the Zambezi leaves and returns to Zambia three times. It enters or borders six different countries, and along its path it variably runs north, south, east, and west.

The southern border of Zambia is formed by the course of the Zambezi which supports all living things. Every year the river floods the land just after it turns east toward its final destination, the Indian Ocean. Thousands of people in the lowlands must migrate seasonally with the floods, escaping to the surrounding hills. During the dry months, the floodplains are rich agricultural land in a part of the world where crops are only irrigated by nature.

AS THEY MOVE THROUGH THE VALLEY, Lua keeps Moyo close for protection, both from the sun and any predators that may be eyeing the vulnerable little elephant. Elephants, the largest animals on earth, the source of life for so many, are always prey and never predator. Lua and Sumina are on perpetual alert. Born with no fear, Moyo trusts without reserve and will do so until she learns otherwise. Fear is something she will be taught by her mother and learn from experience.

For now, Moyo's older brother, Mosi, is her primary playmate. Moyo is too little for roughhousing, but Mosi never turns down a frolic.

He lies on the ground and lets Moyo climb on top of him; she tumbles and rolls down.

Lua observes their play. For an elephant, observing isn't just seeing; she listens, smells, and feels the vibrations of her surroundings. Even with her back turned Lua knows what's happening and stays close. Mosi understands to be gentle. When he's older, this experience will be important if he's around calves. He will be more patient and less likely to hurt them.

Tunya, Moyo's older sister, is also nearby. At nine years, she's healthy and strong, the daughter of an experienced mother. Tunya's job at this stage of life is to learn how to care for young, how to lead a family, how to find food and water, how to respond to predators, and how to communicate. She will need all these skills to be successful in life, especially if she becomes the leader responsible for her family. Older leaders are the most adept at considering the many factors that affect survival. With more experience, the better they are at judging risk and responding to threats.

Today the family heads back toward the trees to rest in the heat of the day when the sun is directly overhead and bakes everything exposed below. In the forest the young ones can take a nap while the older elephants strip small branches or pull up saplings. Their foraging selects out dense undergrowth and provides the larger trees with more nutrients and sunlight, supporting them to grow taller with high treetops or to form canopies. These changes to the woodlands are one reason that birds live where elephants are.

Moyo is too young to eat plants and must rely solely on Lua's milk. At about six months, she will start to pick up scraps from the others. It will be another several months before Moyo watches and imitates the way her mother eats; the careful, rhythmic pulling up of plants and shaking off the soil. Even after Moyo starts to eat, she will nurse for a couple of years. If Lua dies during Moyo's first few years of life, Moyo will almost certainly not survive.

In the late afternoon, the family is active again and moves back toward the open savanna. Another elephant family group is already relaxing there. Lua knows them well, part of her community of elephants that she can recognize by the sound of their voices and address by name. This family is descended from a larger bond group from which Lua's mother split many years ago when the group got too big. Lua approaches the other family from downwind, so she knows they are there long before she sees them, a quality of life for an animal who knows the world by scent or sound.

For Lua, scent information is temporal. Scent contains chemical signals that decay, and the rate of decay informs her about the timing of recent events. From the strength of the scent coupled with the rate of decay, Lua knows the length of time the scent has been in that place. Lua doesn't live in discrete moments the way visually dependent human animals do. Each moment has a temporal aspect of what happened in the past, what is happening now, and what is about to happen, especially if the wind is moving toward her.

As Lua approaches the family leader she trumpets with excitement, but then catches a whiff of anxiety and fear. Kasha is standing still with her tail slack behind her. The two elephants greet each other warmly with salutary rumbles and trunk wraps. Lua touches the sides of Kasha's forehead, where her temporal glands are releasing stress secretions. Kasha's daughter recently gave birth. Lua realizes that Kasha's daughter and her calf aren't there; she cannot find their scents. Lua rumbles softly and touches Kasha's face.

Moyo tussles with another calf. Tunya is wary, the ever-attentive sister, and stays close. The calves are both small; they touch and lie down together, forging friendships that could be valuable later in life. This is how their mothers know each other, from decades of meeting and a history of playing together when they were young.

When Moyo tires, she finds her mother, her most important source of comfort, and lies down next to her. Lua has stayed close to Kasha. The two are standing quietly together without eating. When Moyo wakes, she nurses and then spends some time playing with Mosi. The two families move into a scrubby thicket and share the rest of the afternoon together, foraging on the woody shrubs of the savanna. In the dry season, there is nothing else to eat.

As evening falls, Moyo lies down; her older siblings follow later in the night. In the cool air, the almost full moon disperses light within the scattered clouds. Lions are not on the prowl and the night passes quietly while Moyo sleeps tucked safely under Tunya's chin.

Even for elephants of the savanna, it's been uncomfortably hot during the day. Lua's body self-regulates in response to prevailing conditions, a vital way to save energy for an animal in constant need of calories. During the day her internal temperature may be as high as 99.5 degrees, and overnight it may drop close to 95. The camel, an exemplar of desert animals, has similar adaptations. In places with dry air and ground that radiates sun-drenched heat during the day, overnight temperature drops can be dramatic. The air doesn't retain any of the warmth of the daylight hours and the earth does not reflect the heat. Without an adaptation to cool her internal temperature, Lua would be a giant radiant heater every night, allowing precious energy to escape and dissipate into the expanse of the savanna.

Before the light edges over the horizon at dawn, the soft sounds of the snoring elephants harmonize with the high-pitched trill of the local nightjars. As the young elephants wake and rise, the families perform a ritual of departure with alternating call and response, an elephant conversation.

In a few weeks, Moyo will have a new companion. The little elephant hasn't noticed, but Sumina's belly is getting larger every day. Six years ago, during a drought, Sumina's young calf died when her milk dried up. During that same time the other females didn't go into estrus; hard times will do that. Several years went by without the birth of any calves. But now the family is growing again. Lua and Sumina are not related by biology; theirs is a chosen kinship.

This morning Moyo plays on her own, getting used to her big feet and mock charging birds or small animals. She breaks a stick, and the sound startles her; she trips and tumbles to the ground, then runs squealing back to her mother. Lua appears to be paying little attention to Moyo's antics but knows everything that's happening and is unconcerned by Moyo's squeaky trumpets. When Moyo settles in to nurse, Lua drapes her trunk over Moyo's back, feeling the little one's heartbeat as Moyo calms down.

Unless Lua is resting, her trunk is always in motion. She touches her surroundings, the ground, and other elephants, constantly. Her trunk directs the little ones, calms the distressed, and gathers information. When exploring an object, she may start with her trunk, then rub against it with her sides or flank, and then back up to the object and touch it with her feet. She gets different sensory information from each part of her body.

Lua's vision is better in dim light than in the brightness of day when everything is washed in the sun. In some ways, the light-detecting cells of her eye are similar to aquatic animals, detecting subtle hues and contrasts. Though her visual acuity is lower than ours, especially at a distance further than 46 meters, this doesn't mean that Lua's world lacks detail. She lives in a world of finely perceived scent, sound, and touch.

Sense of smell is difficult to quantify, but Lua has more scent receptors than any other mammal. Elephant lore describes an animal that can smell food or a snake in the grass from a mile away. This chemical-audio-tactile existence shapes everything about how Lua interacts with the world and those around her.

As the family moves together through the trees, they do not need to see each other to keep in contact. Whether among the trees or several kilometers apart, they stay connected through scent and sound, and they remember where each of their family members are—up to seventeen of them according to research. Lua can keep all that spatial information active in her big brain at one time; humans can do this for about seven pieces of information.

If you were in a small plane, high above and looking down, searching for the slow, almost meditative movement of those gray figures, you might see Lua and her family spread out amongst the trees, separate but together. They would be moving in unison, as if they were on parallel tracks across the surface of the earth, even if they were not in sight of the others.

Or if you were closer, sitting in the crook of a high tree in the forest and observing the elephants below, you might see them scattered around, moving in the same direction in silence. You smell their scent like farm animals, huge plant-eaters. But all you would hear is the stripping of bark or the chewing of branches. You might feel them call to each other, a vibration deep in your chest. Their movements are silent; their big, soft feet step without sound. The canopy lets in small beams of sun that move with the branches in the breeze. Dancing light on the forest floor catches your attention. Up in the tree, you startle when you suddenly realize there is a massive animal beneath you, one who seems like a giant boulder that appeared out of nowhere. Lua smelled you long before you knew she was there. And if she still comes near, she has already assessed you and decided that you are not a threat.

If you were standing on the soft forest floor, you might notice something large and dark a few trees away, not sure if it was there a few minutes ago. And then, without warning, Lua is looming over you, all 8,000 pounds of her.

If Lua senses danger, she alerts the others. You can't hear it, but she calls to her family with instructions. Silently they turn together, and then they are gone.

THE 1900S WERE ROUGH FOR ELEPHANTS. *Around one hundred years ago, there were more than five million elephants in Africa. Now the population is estimated at 415,000. Elephants were hunted by Europeans and Americans to near-extinction and extirpated from many areas. This was both for sport and for ivory.*

Theodore Roosevelt famously went on expedition in East Africa, mostly Kenya, in 1909, the same year that his presidency ended. He characterized the journey as one of a great naturalist who had the opportunity to bring some of Africa home for people to see, people who would otherwise never have the chance to experience the wildlife of the continent. While in Eastern and Central Africa, Roosevelt killed 296 large animals and his son killed 216 more.

Though the white rhinoceros was already nearing extinction, Roosevelt shot five and his son shot four, ostensibly to memorialize a bygone era of the natural world. He was motivated to obtain a record of them, by killing them and bringing their bodies to the United States for display before they went extinct. We might consider whether he had an important hand in bringing about that bygone era, a self-fulfilling prophecy. This is the same species which became functionally extinct in the wild in 2014 when the last two wild males died.

The Roosevelts also claimed to have killed eleven elephants, one species out of their total of 76. Even over the last 50 years, the number of savanna elephants across the continent has declined roughly 60 percent. About one hundred each day, which comes to well over 30,000 elephants a year, are killed. Recent reports give a black-market value of up to $375,000 for a pair of tusks.

African forest elephants, the smaller species that is a distant cousin to savanna elephants, are largely relegated to Gabon and the Democratic Republic of the Congo in Central Africa. The elusive and rarely seen forest elephants lost eighty percent of their individuals due to illegal hunting in the early years of the 2000s. They are now considered critically endangered.

Of the savanna elephants that remain, most of them are in Southern Africa. There are still elephants in East Africa, but they have faced even greater challenges. East Africa is geologically distinct from the southern part of the continent. The region has undergone several periods of extreme drought when a significant portion of elephants and other animals were lost. At times hunting rates, both legal and illegal, have also been high there. Though the numbers are better in Southern Africa, the populations are scattered and isolated.

2. *Rain*

DECEMBER

Lua stands with trunk up, taking in the clear air. She spreads her ears out with a crack like a sail catching the wind. The air carries information to her ears and nose. Another morning has broken, and she'll decide on her family's movements, their daily cycle within a larger pattern of the season and even greater revolutions by the year. All animals of Africa are part of this rhythm that marks the passage of time as reliably as the sun.

Heat and rain mark the three distinct seasons here. May to August are the coolest months with dry air that averages around 70 degrees. The hottest, driest season starts in September with an average temperature closer to 90 degrees with highs up to 109. Then the rains break around November, although this transition has been shifting to later in the year. During the rainy season, the heavy air has an average temperature in the upper 70s.

Looking down on this part of the world from above, the earth looks like a quilt of greens and browns. The landscape is put together with patches of spotty scrub brush, grass, sandy washes, scattered trees, and a few forested stands of trees with a closed canopy. Ribbons of green ripple on either side of river tributaries. The rivers here are not straightened or dammed; they snake along the natural features of the valley and the rolling hills to the east.

Even inside the honeypot of the Luangwa Valley, harsh conditions mark the long, dry months. At this time of year, the elephants rely on mopane (the *-ane* is pronounced with an ah sound and a long e, sort of like the *awny* of tawny) trees for their sustenance. The leaves have their autumnal colors now. This happens as the landscape transforms from green to splotches of orange and brown every year during the months of heat. During the dry season, Lua eats more bark than leaves, but her foraging shakes the dried leaves and seed pods to the ground where other wildlife can get them—another reason besides water for small animals to follow the elephants.

Not every year is as difficult as this one, although even an elephant would have a hard time remembering a year that was good. Elephants here have always lived seasonally through wet and dry months but the pervasive heat with the drought it brings every year is a new threat to survival. Lua's mother didn't have to navigate such difficult conditions. In the decades since Lua was born in the honeypot of Zambia, every ten years the temperature has increased by 0.54 degrees Fahrenheit, and the rate of increase continues. Since 1960 there has been an average decrease in annual rainfall of almost two millimeters per decade, with much of this change in the last few years. World maps that depict increases in temperature in red look as though blood has spilled across Sub-Saharan Africa.

Farmers here, like Stary (pronounced like starry) and Mulenga Phiri, are growing fewer crops from the same amount of space. With the rising heat, productivity goes down as the village continues to spread into the surrounding land to provide for the demands of the distant city centers. Like about eighty-five percent of small farm holders in Zambia, the Phiris grow maize for both subsistence and income. Their village in the Luangwa Valley lies within a narrow extension of the agricultural belt of Zambia, which mostly lies along the country's southern border. North of them is arid land and copper mines. Farmers in this part of the world work with a relatively small portion of arable land. At this time of year, Stary and Mulenga have planted their fields. Now they can only hope against the unpredictability of the future.

Stary understands the struggle of the elephants to find water because he knows it too. Every year the ground seems drier, and the rains are more sporadic. Stary has a healthy fear of elephants but also a profound love. He knows how to be safe but sometimes his crops are not. The same year that Sumina lost her baby due to drought, he lost most of his maize to a raiding party of elephants. It was an act of desperation on Lua's part. She did not want to get that close to the village, but they could find nothing else to eat.

It was a devastating loss for Stary and his family. Their year of work and investment was gone. He could not pay his children's school fees for the end of the term, and they all had some hungry days. Stary went without so that his children had more. He was already lithe with long arms and elegant fingers. His body ached from hunger. The community helped as much as they could, but it was a lean year for everyone.

Almost half of the elephants and many other animals died that dry season. The savanna was scattered with carcasses. Only the scavengers looked healthy, but then there was an outbreak of anthrax from contaminated water, a problem related to high rainfall followed by long periods of dry weather. Many of the scavengers died too.

Stary saw the elephants with skin hanging loosely around their faces. Their hips stuck out. Other plant-eaters of the area did not fare any better. The impala looked thin, and their coats were dull. Stary knew that the elephants could find no other food than what he and his family had toiled to grow, no choice. His wife, Mulenga, was not so forgiving until Stary determined a plan to protect their crops from elephants in the future.

A few years ago, some researchers came to the area to test ways for farmers to keep elephants out of their fields. Around the crops they hung ropes that were covered in a mixture of chile paste and engine oil. Elephants don't like chile. Other farmers tried chile smoke briquettes—made from a mixture of dried chiles and elephant dung. The briquettes are placed on fires at the corners of the fields overnight to make an acrid chile smoke. In some places the researchers hung cow bells around the fields. Some farmers were given banger sticks made locally with match heads on the ends to make noise. Most crop-raiding happens at night; sleeping in the fields and scaring away elephants with noise or light is a tradition in some places. In two villages the researchers built watchtowers and gave the farmers flashlights—some elephants are deterred by a single directed light. The researchers instructed the volunteers to make sure their deterrents did not block the elephant paths because that could increase the conflict instead of reducing it. It could also keep the elephants from getting to water. In some of the villages people asked to try beehive fences to scare away the elephants and harvest the honey, but hives were too expensive and difficult to obtain.

All the solutions reduced crop-raiding, but none were simple or easy to maintain. The match head sticks were stopped because in some places theft by humans was worse than theft by elephants, and local authorities were concerned about encouraging confrontations between people. Many of the flashlights broke, and the cowbells were taken for domestic animals. The chile paste and engine oil rope was considered a success but making the paste and reapplying it was too labor intensive. The chile-elephant dung briquettes were also time consuming but seemed to be the easiest to keep going—an irony of using elephants' own waste as a defense against them.

After the researchers left, Stary heard about keeping elephants away with chile plants, not only the paste. During the next season of planting, he planted chile pepper seeds among the maize. He got the seeds on loan with an agreement to pay back the debt when he harvested his maize at the end of the season.

Maybe the peppers kept the elephants away or maybe they didn't, but the elephants haven't returned, and Mulenga is happy. Every year, Stary has grown more peppers and now plants them around the entire perimeter of his fields. Mulenga also uses them for cooking, and Stary can barter at the market with the extra peppers.

WEEKS LATER THAN EXPECTED, there's a change in the air. The rains have broken in the south, and in her mysterious elephant way, Lua can sense the storms up to 150 miles in the distance. She heads out with her family to meet the rain that moves toward them. As they travel, they make low rumbling noises to keep in contact with each other. Those infrasonic sounds are too low for human animals to hear which serves our illusion of elephant silence. Today the air is still and heavy, saturated with moisture that is almost thick enough to precipitate and fall. They walk together as a procession with Lua, the leader, bringing up the rear.

During the dry months, Lua's family finds its home along the tributaries of the Luangwa River, but after the rains soak the earth and the landscape returns to green, their routes open. They become travelers again, to roam the elephant paths used for millennia across the surface of Africa. Lua follows the water and the food without concern for arbitrary political borders we would find on a map, but when a border demarcates a region that is unsafe for elephants, Lua understands.

Moyo keeps up but still needs rest and cannot cross large rivers. Lua knows how to plan a path that Moyo can manage. Other than that, her only limitations are the terrain that they can handle and knowing where humans are. As human boundaries are perpetually expanding, Lua's choices are decreasing, and her routes must change.

Lua's deliberate nature is about much more than the time it takes to get that big body to move. She was built for a contemplative, graceful pace of life. Lua's brain structure favors long-term memory over speed of processing. Having the largest brain of any land animal means having the longest neurons. The speed of neural signaling is related to the length and density of the cell's conduction fibers; signals take longer to travel the length of Lua's neurons. This is part of the reason that the scale of time is different for an elephant: they process information slowly. Both neural transmission and metabolism are slower. Relatively poor eyesight may play a role as well. Chemical and auditory senses may simply require more processing time or interpretation.

Lua also communicates over large distances, through the ground, a slow medium. Her massive chest and ability to push out an enormous amount of air mean that she can produce very low frequency sounds, even lower than her eardrum's capacity to detect. Why would she be able to produce a sound that her ear can't hear?

When a wave of sound reaches Lua, it passes through her ear canal to her tympanic membrane and then into the middle ear, where a chain of three small bones called ossicles turn the sound frequency into vibrations that are passed to the inner ear. This process is the same in humans, but Lua's eardrums and ossicles are huge. Even when the overall size of her skull is considered, her ossicles are ten times larger than those of any human. This anatomy increases conduction of sound by her bones, especially at low frequencies, which also heightens her ability to detect sound over a distance.

Sound is a wave of physical energy that moves through space before dissipating. This process can change with objects in the way and whether they absorb or reflect the waves. High frequency sounds run into objects and lose energy, but low frequency sounds, with waves meters apart, can bypass objects altogether and travel much farther. This difference is even more pronounced through the ground than the air, seismic rather than acoustic transmission.

Lua's feet, her seismic detectors, look clumsy and cloddy. Though her toes are not dexterous, or even obvious without a close look, her feet are part of what makes her so sensitive to the world around her. X-rays would show that she stands on her toes, like a giant ballerina, with bones at the front of her foot. The rear of her foot is a thick, dense pad of fat, which conducts vibrations like ripples moving across water.

It also makes her footfalls incredibly quiet, softly cushioning her weight against the earth with every step.

The fat pad is similar in structure to the acoustic fat of marine mammals such as dolphins, whose fat pad in their foreheads propagates sound waves to the bony structures of the ear. Lua's foot pad squishes against the earth, vibrations go to the bones of her foot, then up her leg bones, shoulder, and ultimately to her inner ear. Lua can hear vibrations from her feet. The vibrations reach Lua's consciousness, helping her find water underground and communicate with other elephants more than six miles away. She can sense the movement of her children at play or recognize the sound of vehicles. If an animal is close enough, she can identify what kind of animal it is. But it's not a perfect system. Lua can still be startled by animals who don't make the earth vibrate, especially when it's windy.

Lua can purposefully amplify the vibrations from her feet by contracting muscles at the opening of her ear canals, similar to when a person pushes her ears closed to hear her own voice better. The effect increases bone conduction of sound waves to the inner ear and decreases interference from ambient noise in her surroundings. This helps Lua to detect subtle sounds that she picks up as vibrations.

Both Lua's trunk tip and feet also have direct vibration sensors. These specialized nerve cells have a direct pathway to her brain, unlike the fat pad which sends vibration information to her ear before it gets to her brain. She can place her trunk tip on the ground and detect distinct vibrations from hooves, feet, and vehicles—or do this through her feet. The direct-to-the-brain cells are clustered mostly at the front and back of Lua's foot and are organized in fine, discrete layers, like an onion. When ground vibrations move across these rows of cells, away from the source of the vibration, a signal is sent to her brain. Sometimes when Lua is considering a decision, she shifts silently on her feet, actively collecting information about the world around her.

Fat pads in her feet, muscular ear plugs, and wave detecting nerve cells all amplify vibration information, essentially making her a giant vibration-sensing creature, sensitive to alterations of waves. Lua can literally feel disturbances of energy in the air or the ground.

Lua's mental representation of the geography of her life, her navigational foundation, was formed by years of experiences and long-term sensory memory. She understands the world through the smells, tastes, sounds, sights, and touches of her history, which she can compare with what is happening now. It is a visceral relationship between animal and land that forms an internal map of sensation that she applies as she moves across hundreds of miles of savanna.

Knowing the land by her senses means that Lua relies on different landmarks than humans use. As Lua walks, her nose is active near the ground. She can monitor her world as if she is a mongoose of the savanna floor, tracking what has happened on the soil. But she also monitors the world with her ears up at ten feet in the air, like antennae collecting sound. Though her central vision lacks fine detail, her eyes are sensitive for detecting movement on her periphery, especially predators.

Lua integrates those vibrations and scents with shadows and subtle hues of blues, yellows, and browns, both to monitor her surroundings and to navigate the landscape. When she needs more information from the air, she stands with her head back, trunk up, and ears out, taking in all the smells and sounds she can gather. When she needs more information from the ground, she sniffs or puts the tip of her trunk, with its delicate sensory cells, on the earth.

At its highest point, Victoria Falls measures at 355 feet, which is the equivalent of a 35-story building. It is also more than a mile wide. During the rainy season, all this water plunges into the raging gorge below at more than 300,000 gallons per second. When conditions are right, the thundering cascade of the falls can be heard by humans as far away as 25 miles. If humans can hear Victoria Falls, "The Smoke that

Thunders," from 25 miles away, how far away could Lua feel it through the ground? From how far away could she use the world's best ground-level navigational reference point?

Lua's constant sensation from and awareness of her surroundings is how she monitors her family and their safety as they travel. At her size, lions are the primary threat to Moyo. Even young elephants can tell the difference in the vocalizations from a single versus multiple lions; groups are a much more serious threat. But an experienced leader like Lua can also tell the difference between male and female lion calls. There are subtle acoustic differences in the calls of male and female lions, so subtle that they are missed by human ears. Even if lionesses are superior hunters, male lions are much larger and more of a threat to young elephants. Unless the elephant is separated from its mother, there must be several females to be much of a menace, but males are dangerous on their own.

If she heard a male lion, Lua would immediately call for a bunch-and-defend strategy with the young ones in the center of the group. They would also remain on alert for longer than if the call was from a lioness. Or if the lions are very close, mob-and-attack is a better defense. Older leaders are better and quicker at making these decisions. Tunya stays nearby to learn from her mother and help.

THE ELEPHANTS MOVE AT A SLOW AND STEADY PACE. As they pass along the eastern edge of the valley, the wind picks up and ripples through the lowlands between the rolling hills and the mountains. They have been walking toward the dark sky, and the air is thick. Flashes of lightning reveal silvery outlines from the wall of clouds. Lua can feel the thunder and tell where the storm front is moving. All the elephants smell the rain long before they feel its splashes.

The first drops are big and heavy; each one hits the elephants with a splatter. Before long, water tumbles from the sky in a deluge, and there are rivulets at their feet. It takes time for the ground beneath them to soften and accept the water. The soil releases that sweet, earthy smell, so powerful after seven months with no rain. It won't be long before the brown hillsides burst with color on an emerald backdrop. Clusters of delicate flowers on the forest floor will bloom yellow, dusky red, and white.

Lua keeps her family out in the open, away from trees to avoid lightning. This is Moyo's first rain. At first, she tucks underneath her mother's body while the older elephants delight in being drenched, as elephants do. Elephants love rain; they love water. They raise their faces and flap their ears like big gray butterflies as their skin darkens. Sumina stands in front of Lua, and they wrap trunks in an elephant embrace. All of them are calling and trumpeting. Moyo gets braver and steps into the downpour. She splashes in the water at her feet. Even Tunya, the serious one, runs and hip-checks Mosi. She is feeling elephant joy. He pushes back and they tussle as the family shares these moments together to delight in the water and the changing of seasons.

Zambia, the family's home, is nearly split in the middle by a portion of the Democratic Republic of the Congo that extends southward. It gives Zambia the appearance of lobes, like a helicopter seed falling from a maple tree. Zambia has several metropolitan areas. The largest is the capital, Lusaka, an international city that lies between the two lobes of the country. Along the eastern side of Zambia, more than 400 miles from Lusaka, the Muchinga escarpment extends at a diagonal north-south. This is the area where the drainage basin of the Zambezi River separates from that of the Congo to the north. Within this geographical formation, there are more than three hundred named mountain peaks. East of the escarpment is the Luangwa Valley, a place whose identity is determined by the time of year. In other words, at any given time it is more or less of a swamp. Along the eastern edge of the valley is the Luangwa River. At its lowest point, the valley is just over 1,500 feet in elevation. The highest Muchinga peaks are more than 5,500 feet. The east face of the escarpment is very steep.

The equatorial zone of Africa runs through this area where the trade winds of the north meet those of the south. This land in-between can be the site of heavy storms and high clouds, shifting with the seasons. It is also the land of the doldrums, the still air hated by soldiers which has become a euphemism for low spirits.

Usually, the higher air is, the colder it is. But on a cloudless and windless night, a warm layer can develop in-between the ground and an upper layer of cool air. This is important to Lua because sound travels differently when this warm duct is in the middle. The speed of sound is faster at higher temperatures, so when sound travels up from the earth it moves quickly within this warm layer before eventually being reflected back down by the cool air above. Under these conditions, Lua's calls carry much farther than otherwise. The effect is exaggerated when there are obstacles at ground level because the sound is not absorbed or dissipated at those spots. It is as if her rumbles jump across the earth.

Dusk and dawn favor this phenomenon, allowing Lua to communicate with unseen elephants over long distances. She can feel the movement of human animals in vehicles, especially the noisy start to their day. As night falls, this is the best time for humans to hear the elephants rumbling long and low to each other, with voices that carry over hills and human developments. Perhaps they are relaying events of the day or warnings, another way of keeping each other safe.

Now that the rains have arrived, Lua finds better food. During the dry season, eating a lot of woody bushes and branches is part of their elephant job in a natural cycle of depletion and growth. Clearing out fibrous plants, which other animals can't eat, allows grasses to grow. Zebra, wildebeest, gazelle, buffalo, giraffe, impala, and others all rely on the savanna for grass. Predators that eat these grass-eaters also rely on the savanna as a place to hunt. Forest dwellers, grass-eaters, and predators all need the elephants. And in turn, other herbivores eat the grasses and allow the woody brush to grow for the elephants to eat when the grass is too dry for them. It's a balance of living things, each with their part to play.

When the earth is soft from rain, Lua's big, heavy body and flat feet make puddles. Those round puddles support a bounty of creatures, including insects and amphibians. In some places, elephants create the primary environment for breeding and the beginnings of life for these small animals. At times of the year when everything else has evaporated, their footprint puddles are the only cups that hold water.

Elephants are messy eaters, leaving behind detritus where frogs or lizards can hide and breed, or shelter their young. In the forest they clear paths in the dense undergrowth that are essential for smaller animals to move within. As they travel the family leaves habitats in their wake—habitats that are more varied and complex in their presence than without them, which means that they support a greater biodiversity.

At the height of the rainy season when the land is swampy, the tributaries of the Luangwa rush with muddy water and the roads wash out. No amount of road grading can protect the surface from the force and stamina of the rainy season torrent. For weeks, Lua and her family traveled south in parallel with the river. Now they move west into a strip of veld before the slopes of the mountains begin their ascent.

Overnight, mist settles into the lowlands. Every dawn exposes features of the foothills where the low passageways between forest slopes are still thick with fog as sunlight first makes its way over the horizon. During the day these corridors are hidden in plain sight, the failure of the eyes to differentiate one tree-covered slope from the next.

Tender, wet, pink shoots of grass shine with dew each morning, and the trees are green with fresh foliage. The marula has borne its prized fruit, a favorite of human and nonhuman animals, especially elephants—which gives it the moniker *elephant tree*.

Ripe marula fruit, otherwise known as cat thorn or jelly plum, has a fleshy white meat on the inside and a pale-yellow outside. A relative of the mango, marula is a stone fruit with a pit in the center about the size of a walnut. The fruit falls from the tree when it's still green, and the meat is firm. It ripens on the ground where most animals pick it up. Elephants prefer the immature fruit, still green on the tree.

If animals do not get them first, people can harvest the marula for food and for sale, an important source of income for some people in rural communities. In addition to eating the fruit, the juice and pulp can be mixed with water and fermented into marula wine, or it can be made into a cream liquor called Amarula. Animals, through gut fermentation, turn the fruit, especially the ripe fruit, into alcohol. This is part of the legend of drunken elephants, which has some basis in reality, as elephants have been known to drink alcohol meant for human consumption. Though not impossible, intoxication by marula is improbable. They would have to eat enough marula to generate several liters of alcohol, which would take so long that they couldn't absorb and retain enough to feel drunk.

Despite the implausibility that elephants get drunk on marula, it's still a favorite food source for the brief period that it's available. Its seed passes through an elephant in one piece, ready to germinate far from the tree that spawned it. All part of the living work of elephants.

The family approaches a water hole where wildebeest are drinking and loitering. As the elephants move in, the wildebeest move aside in deference. Lua takes the first drink as Moyo moves in and crouches beneath her, allowed at the front of the line. The other elephants take their turns at the water's edge, enjoying the beginning of the season and the fresh water. Soon rain will come more regularly, and they sense the change in the air with relief.

Mosi is tempted to get into the shallow pool and wallow as elephants do, but he must wait until they are done drinking. Otherwise, he will get scolded for mucking up the water. Instead, he runs around the edge of the pool and chases a young wildebeest who is not interested in playing. Mosi finds a warthog and charges him, then swerves away. The two animals posture toward each other and take turns chasing and fleeing.

The warthog grunts in excitement, and Mosi makes a ruckus, finding his adult trumpet and flapping his ears. This goes on until Mosi gets too close and the warthog gives Mosi a little poke with his sharp tusks. Mosi runs animatedly back to Lua who does not seem impressed by his injury.

The family relaxes at the edge of the water until Lua signals them to go. She felt the approach of elephant bulls who appear like six boulders moving across the horizon. Lua moves her family before the bulls arrive at the water. Mosi starts to follow but then stops in curiosity and waits off to the side. He watches as the largest, oldest bull steps to the best spot at the water's edge. The five younger bulls fill in around him, touching the older bull's mouth while he is drinking. After a long drink, in silence and grace, the big bull walks away. Though his legs move slowly, he covers ten feet with every stride. As he reaches the edge of the pan, the younger bulls stop drinking or wallowing and surreptitiously walk in his direction.

Lua and the rest of the family have gone. Mosi follows in the direction they went. He runs and bellows as though he is afraid of being abandoned, but it's not hard for him to call and find his mother. Mosi rejoins the family as they are resting, preparing to follow the rain again—the difference between life and death.

AT LEAST 200 MILLION YEARS AGO, *most of earth's landmass existed as a single continent. Africa, Europe, South America, and North America formed a contiguous landmass that geologists call Pangea. Tectonic movement pulled Pangea apart into the continents that we know today with a force that never stopped. A rift under East Africa continues to separate the continent into smaller landmasses at an incomprehensible few millimeters per year. Someday new oceans will form, and new islands will be cast into the Indian Ocean.*

African savanna elephants have existed as the species that we know for three million years or more. In a little over one hundred years, we have managed to directly threaten their existence in waves of attack and regress. Our history of killing, then protecting elephants, has taken them to the precipice and back, but this history is much simpler than the problems that elephants face now—conflict with humans and a heating earth.

Until temperatures reach a breaking point that is incompatible with life, the heat will continue to amplify conflict between humans and elephants, with more competition for water and elephants looking for cultivated food when other sources fail. Elephants have survived this long because of their intelligence and adaptability to changing conditions, but neither animals nor plants can adapt to temperatures rising so fast. Elephants cannot survive having nowhere to go, nothing to eat or drink.

Climate variability brings drought and flood. Both of these are driven by heat, and both are increasing in frequency and intensity. If unabated, the escalating rise in temperature will make much of Southern Africa uninhabitable in the next couple of decades.

Earth's atmosphere, glaciers, oceans, life as we know it—things that we consider permanent—are changing around us. We struggle to comprehend how our actions could possibly affect natural phenomena so much bigger than we are, or distant people in faraway and unfamiliar places.

Some scientists believe that understanding our natural world within the historical context of extreme long-term, such as billions of years, can increase mindfulness of humanity's role on earth. It can be mind-expanding in that we feel more connected to people of both the distant past and the far-reaching future. We might even better comprehend the consequences of our actions around the world now—for our human and nonhuman kin. Perhaps considering natural events in the extreme long term helps remove these processes from the context and limits of our own ephemeral lives.

3. *New Life*

JANUARY

Sumina is visibly pregnant. After 22 months of gestation, the baby will be born ready to walk, travel, and play with Moyo. It will have no real infancy. When Sumina begins to feel the contractions, she finds Lua, who already recognizes by scent that something has changed. They know the birth is imminent and stop in a small stand of trees surrounded by tall grass.

Lua stands close and keeps Sumina calm. She touches Sumina's face and speaks to her with soothing rumbles. Tunya hovers, curious about what's happening while she keeps an eye on Moyo. Mosi stays foraging nearby. They all monitor for activity in the tall grass—dubbed *adrenaline grass* by scouts because you never know what might be lurking there, ready to pounce or charge.

After the baby drops, Sumina and Lua rumble excitedly. Tunya, a supportive auntie, circles and touches Rumphi. This won't change much as Rumphi grows. He will learn about the world surrounded by family and other elephants who care for and take care of him. Using their trunks and gentle nudges with their feet, within half an hour Sumina and Lua have encouraged him to stand up. Soon after, he nurses while Sumina touches him gently with her trunk. In an hour Rumphi is walking. Lua will give him a couple of easy days, but then he must be ready to travel.

Right now, Rumphi and Moyo are all legs and clumsy, big feet. As they grow, they'll get taller and broader; they won't change color. They won't gain spots or lose spots. Their ears will not pop up or flop down. No one looks at a baby elephant and is confused about what species it might be. Elephants are born as goofy, little (it's all relative), tubs of energy. The physical changes that they go through as they age mostly involve mastery of their huge bodies, and how to use incoming sensory information, rather than changes in the appearance of their physical selves.

Lua is the largest elephant in her family, though Mosi will outgrow her soon. She has long, striking tusks; one of them is crooked, bending up and sideways. The edges of her ears are just beginning to show the wear and tear of age that makes an old elephant's ears look like ragged fabric. Lua's physical presence and the way she carries herself announce that she is in charge. She bears the experiences of her life with her, those experiences which have made her patient and confident but also wary and careful.

Elephants with long tusks, nearly hitting the ground, used to be common in Africa. This gene has largely been removed by hunters who selected their prey for the biggest trophy, the largest "ivory harvest." Big tuskers are now rare. Sumina never developed visible tusks at all, an adaptation to that hunting selection pressure and the result of a genetic bottleneck where isolated populations develop characteristics not common elsewhere. Tuskless elephants used to be rare in Africa, but no longer. Not having tusks might save Sumina's life, but in other ways, such as protection from predators or ability to dig, she is more vulnerable without them.

Moyo and Rumphi will learn to use their trunks for drinking, then other control will develop over a few years. Though the trunk has eight muscles, the muscles have further subdivisions of function—about 90,000 bundles. Lua's trunk has no bones or cartilage but is so strong that she can easily throw a grown man into the air. At the end of her trunk are two fingers she uses in opposition, like our thumb and forefinger.

Nerves in her trunk tip are similar to those in our fingers, picking up information about texture, shape, temperature, vibration, and feeling pain. Her trunk is so dexterous she could pick up a grain of rice or a dime lying flat on the floor.

Lua can pull her trunk muscles together lengthwise, or let them relax, with an up and down movement. Her complex vocalizations are possible in part because of this ability to lengthen or shorten her trunk. She can also modify sound by constricting the trunk diameter at various points, curve it up in an "S" or hold it straight out. The word trunk originates from the French word for trumpet, *trompe*. Of course, sound does not originate in the trunk, it's like the trumpet played by the trumpeter. With a larynx more complex than ours, Lua can change the shape of her throat to vary her expressions. She can make more than thirty distinct vocal sounds and modify the meaning of those sounds with visual signals, body language, and touch. Like our tone of voice, her calls also carry emotional information, and she can make novel sounds by combining her basic vocalizations. All this complexity and variability helps Lua communicate specific meaning, to organize the family as a unit.

Lua learned all of this from her mother and her family. Having a close relationship with older females is essential for adolescent elephants. They must learn to receive and convey meaning. Tunya makes a careful study of it all. Her brain will continue growing up to the age of fifteen, much like our brain growth until the age of sixteen. Someday the family will depend on Tunya, who is learning to read the land and other animals by paying close attention to her mother. She saw how her mother helped during Rumphi's birth. Lua teaches by both example and instruction, in that mysterious way of elephants.

DURING SUMINA'S FIRST PREGNANCY, hunters killed her mother and aunt. The men were waiting and startled them from behind a rock outcropping. They were too close for the family to flee, so Sumina's mother and aunt charged and were immediately shot. One of the men was a professional hunter who knew how to get away with killing an elephant without a license.

The rest of Sumina's family turned and ran for as long as they could. The surviving elephants were young and inexperienced. Without a leader they did not know how to navigate and wandered aimlessly, hoping to find food and water. Her brother was little and though he had already weaned, was still dependent on his mother. He was starving and weak when the group tried to cross a river that was too fast for him. Sumina was naïve and did not realize that he was not big enough or strong enough until it was too late. As he struggled, the others attempted to help him across. He followed close to their cousin while Sumina tried to hold him up from behind, but he was washed downstream and drowned.

Not long after, Sumina had her first baby. Without an experienced female around to guide and comfort her, she was confused and distressed. She did not know what was happening until the baby dropped from her. She was standing in the open, exposed to the sun and did not shade him or help him stand. Hours later, when he finally figured it out on his own, Sumina did not know how to position herself so that he could nurse. Female elephants have two mammary glands between their front legs, on their chests, very much like humans. A mother must stand with a foot forward for her baby to reach up and nurse. First-time mothers can use help in getting this right.

Sumina struggled to find food and water. She had not yet learned the routes that her mother had learned from her grandmother. Her baby, entirely dependent on her milk, was starving but was killed by a lioness before he could die from dehydration or starvation. He was an easy target as he failed to keep up. A group of lionesses surrounded the indecisive group of young elephants who did not know how to work together to protect the baby.

Sumina separated from her small family and hid in the forest to grieve. It is impossible to know if she would have survived this event.

Sometimes elephants in captivity die shortly after experiencing sudden loss of a close companion. Caretakers might say that they died of a broken heart—a phenomenon not unheard of in humans. Or Sumina might simply have not been able to survive on the savanna alone, but after languishing for several days, Lua's family passed by and Sumina followed them. She stayed at a distance for several weeks, close enough to eat and drink after them. Over time, Lua approached Sumina and welcomed her to the family. Lua could sense Sumina's unrelenting fear and sorrow.

Sumina and Lua have been companions, a bonded pair, for more than a decade. Lua's early life with her mother is the foundation of her calm and confidence. Sumina's life has made her nervous and skittish, but she is getting better. After years of infertility from elevated stress hormones, Sumina went into estrus again and had a second baby. He died during a drought because Sumina could not feed him. His little skeleton rests in an open area near the family's dry season home. When they are close, Sumina visits his bones and touches them. Sometimes she picks up his skull and carries it for a little while, but she always gently returns it to the spot where he lays. Now she has another chance, another son to care for.

The rain is more consistent during this time of year, and food and water will be enough for a few months. Fruit comes into season, and Lua knows exactly where to find it. Mangoes are ripe to the south, reason enough to traverse miles and put her family near humans—although only those she trusts. Every year she stoically leads them through the lobby of a tourist lodge in the Luangwa Valley to get to the mangoes on the other side. Her mother made this journey before her, and her mother's mother before that. They walk past respectful staff and amazed tourists, careful not to disturb anything as they pass.

Lua knows the humans by smell and by sound, which ones are risky, and which are not. Tourist trucks have a characteristic way of stopping and starting, stopping and starting, sometimes similar to mosquitoes buzzing around her. The tourists also make noise in different ways than locals, talking openly, sometimes loudly near the animals. Though they can be annoying, they also mark the areas that Lua knows are safe. For the human animals of her home range, Lua knows the speech patterns of those who hunt elephants and those who do not. Or she can tell by scent which humans are dangerous. She also knows the voices of women and children, who are usually safe, though not always.

SOMETIMES STARY SEES ELEPHANTS on the edge of the village, especially near the National Park boundary. He loves to listen to their sounds, their contented chuffs and see the way they interact with each other. Seeing them always makes him feel closer to his father. Stary and his wife did not grow up around elephants, as it was a time of rampant hunting. But when his father, Chilu, was a boy, elephants were plentiful, and he learned a deep reverence for them.

Chilu told stories about elephants, not myths or legends, but real experiences from his childhood. He could imitate the sounds an elephant makes and explain what they mean. He recognized when an elephant was angry and threatening to charge. He knew how to avoid startling them and triggering an attack. Chilu taught Stary all of this and passed on his love for elephants and other animals, though elephants were special to him because he felt they were like humans in many ways.

When Chilu was about eight years old, he went to play near the river on an oppressively hot day. Clambering on some rocks, he saw a family of elephants nearby, quietly drinking. Several of the older elephants were keeping an eye on Chilu but didn't look worried and showed no signs of aggression. At that age, he already knew how to keep a safe distance. If needed, he could scale up the rocks where the elephants wouldn't follow.

Chilu was playing with a stick in the sand and watching the elephants when he disturbed a spitting cobra who had been hiding under a rock. He saw the sudden movement of the snake and jumped back, letting out a yelp of fear. He was now on the open sand. The snake was not in pursuit but was holding its ground by rearing up and flaring its hood. One of the elephants ran toward Chilu and the snake, quickly picked up a rock with the tip of her trunk and hurled it like an underhand pitch at the cobra. Her first throw was high, but she corrected, and her second throw hit the snake squarely. The cobra slithered away, and Chilu stood there dumbfounded as the elephant turned and walked calmly back to her family.

Elephants don't like snakes either.

Stary felt that his father owed his life to that elephant, and by extension his life as well. As a child, Stary had a pet starling. He found the young bird with a damaged wing and nursed her back to health. She went everywhere with him and even met him after school each day. The bird brought him things from the trees that he could not reach, like nuts or fruit. He taught her to play hide-and-seek with a button that she brought him. At first, Stary was always the hider, and the starling was the seeker. Then the starling started to take her turn, hiding the button from Stary. The bird understood his perspective. She knew how to put the button in a place where he could not see her or the button, but where he would be able to find it. One day the starling did not meet him after school, and Stary never saw her again.

During those years, many things in Stary's life were unpredictable. The village had no reliable water source. Every day his mother and aunt spent hours walking to the river to retrieve water. During the driest part of the season, when the water was low, they had to hope there were enough elephants around to dig fresh wells. If not, they might not find water at all. Plus, crocodiles can't hide in elephant wells.

One year, some foreigners came to build wells with pumps in each of the villages of the area. There was a meeting for the whole regional community, to discuss the plan and introduce the people who were going to oversee the work. With a village well, life was much easier for his mother. Everything was good for a while, but the organization ran out of money and closed down before the plan was finished for all of the villages.

Neighboring villagers started coming every day to his village to get their water. It was closer and safer than walking to the river. The water flow from the pump became much weaker and soon there were arguments over the water. His village assigned a guard to the pump, to protect the water from anyone who did not live there. The women stopped coming, but the animosity between the villages has never completely gone away and the other village has not prospered, a strange phenomenon for a culture based on sharing and cooperating.

NOW THAT RUMPHI HAS ARRIVED, a sweet and shy companion, Moyo has a playmate of her size, although he will quickly overtake her if he gets good nutrition. Rumphi's experience of life is completely different from that of Sumina's first calf. He is surrounded by elephants who touch and comfort, who constantly monitor the surroundings and keep him safe. Lua knows where to go so that his mother has the best chance to find enough food.

Mosi is beginning to stay on the edge of the group. In a couple of years, by the age of fifteen, they may not see him much at all. With more time on his own he can stray from the family to find extra food. He still has a lot of growing to do. Mosi lived through several dry seasons as a small calf. Even after his most vulnerable first years had passed, the family had a hard time finding food. During those years, there were many hunters in the area, looking for ivory or other trophies. Lua was forced to keep the family within a small portion of the National Park where they were safer. Between so many elephants trapped in its boundaries and the dry conditions, much of the vegetation died.

Though Mosi survived those difficult early years, his life expectancy is likely shorter than it would be otherwise. Adversity during development can cause permanent changes to DNA, leading to errors in cell division, a fundamental process of life. Both human and nonhuman animals have telomere segments at the end of each chromosome that protect DNA when it is copied. As an animal ages, these segments shorten, and the cell becomes inactive or dies. Telomere shortening can also be caused by physical or emotional stress, especially in the young. Affected individuals are not as robust and can even pass these changes to their offspring.

Mosi will be more susceptible to infectious disease and have lower tolerance for challenges such as drought or lack of food. He's already a magnificent creature but may never develop into the grand bull that his father was. All Mosi can do to grow and thrive is eat as much as possible. For now, he's still his mother's child. As long as he stays near, he continues to learn where to go, how to find food and water, and how to be safe, especially at night.

As protector of life, Lua is responsible for her family, but by eating, walking, and defecating across Africa they also make it possible for other animals to live. In addition to clearing woody shrubs, digging water holes, and leaving footprint puddles and other habitats as they travel from one region to another, they leave behind seeds primed to germinate in the nutrients left behind.

About half of what Lua eats stays undigested and becomes massive, steamy piles of seeds and fertilizer. Elephants eat more and travel farther than any other animal, but their importance goes beyond the simple distance of transport. Some seeds will not germinate without passing through Lua's bowels; other animals simply do not prime seeds in this same, necessary way. The landscape and elephants of Africa evolved in dual reliance. Elephants need the food; plant seeds need the priming and dispersal.

Rumphi is only a few days old when the family approaches a large water hole one evening as the sun is sinking in the west, and the horizon looks like a watercolor painting swathed in a broad stripe of orange underneath an impossibly rich blue sky. In the shadow of the mountains and the glow of the sky, the water turns into a mirror, reflecting silhouettes of animals around the pool and the shiny bumps of partially submerged hippos. The hippos occasionally burst with their loud grunting and honking sounds that skitter over the water. Zebras and impalas are jumbled together at the edge of the pool. Lua knows crocodiles are there, hidden underneath the water.

Lua is still at a distance from the activity of the water hole when she halts. The family waits quietly while she is searching for a scent in the shifting wind. Sumina moves Rumphi underneath her body. Suddenly the baboons screech in alarm and scamper toward the trees. They have seen something that Lua hasn't sensed, but now she knows for certain that there are lions nearby. Two females make their move from behind a stand of grass, and the impalas and zebras turn to run. Lua, Sumina, Mosi, and Tunya form a ring around Moyo and Rumphi, but they are not the object of the lionesses' attention. The two cats leap toward the impalas but quickly run out of steam. It seems a half-hearted chase of the scattering antelopes before the lionesses give up and wander off. They are not hungry enough for a big effort.

The family waits until the lions have moved on. Finally, Lua directs Moyo to the shallow edge with a gradual, sandy slope into the water. Rumphi goes to the edge at a deeper spot with a small drop-off at the bank. Sumina does not realize that she needs to stop him and make him wait until it is too late. When he crouches and submerges his mouth to get a drink, his little body tumbles forward into the water. He can stand but the water reaches near the top of his head. He can't get out and doesn't know how to use his trunk like a snorkel.

Sumina panics, tries to hook her trunk behind his front legs and pull him out. Lua leaves Tunya to watch over Moyo while she runs to help. Lua eases into the water and pushes the little elephant from behind. Rumphi reaches his feet to the bank but then topples backward. Sumina gently lifts his trunk from the water so he can breathe while Lua repositions herself. Eventually, Lua gets underneath Rumphi and pushes him up enough for him to plant his feet and climb out of the water. Sumina guides him with her trunk. Lua clambers out after him, and everyone is safe.

After Rumphi's scare at the water hole, the family stops near some trees for the remainder of the day. The young elephant is still scared and tired and only wants to lie underneath his mother, who stands quietly over him. Sumina tremors while Lua touches and comforts her. Finally, Sumina calms down. As darkness falls, the night savanna awakens around them.

Animals own the night. When advantage favors those who know the world by sound and scent, humans are left in the dark. Many animals of this part of the world are nocturnal, out in the openness of the savanna under every star in the night sky of the southern hemisphere and the stars of other galaxies. If they are hungry enough, lions will hunt during the day, but they are the masters of the night. Even a full moon can take away their advantage. Darker is better—their eyes can capture enough light from the shimmering stars. Prey species who can't see well in the dark have techniques for night defense. Hooved animals like impalas or wildebeest bunch together. Most primates, like baboons or vervet monkeys, head to the trees.

In the remote places of Southern Africa, artificial light doesn't pollute the night, and the moon's features command greater attention than in many parts of the world. Once upon a time, the moon asked the hare to tell humans that she had died but rose again, so humans should die and rise again. After the hare failed to deliver the correct message, the moon was angry and the two of them fought. The hare kicked and scratched, leaving marks on her face. Or there was a king who tried to capture the moon for his spoiled son who already had everything else. The king built a ladder to reach the moon, but as he got to the top, he stumbled and his shoulder pushed through the moon's soft surface, leaving a mark.

Sounds of the savanna come alive in the darkness. A lion's roar can be heard by humans from five miles away, while their soft, throaty chuff means they are close by. Spotted hyenas laugh their high-pitched cackle, usually heard when they are on the run from a predator. They also whoop to each other over distances, especially before or after an attack. The large-eyed bushbaby cries disconcertingly like a human infant. Animals of the savanna know when an elephant is born, or the lions have a successful hunt. They know when a wildebeest is caught, a community of predator and prey, big and small. It's a dynamic balance of living things developed over millennia, largely thanks to the ecosystem caretaking of elephants.

Lua is cathemeral, living without clear day and night rhythm. As an animal who does not rely on vision, lack of light does not change her behavior much. The heat of the sun is more important to Lua than the light of the day or dark of the night.

OVER THE NEXT WEEKS, the family continues to follow the rain under Lua's attentive care as they move south. They travel parallel to the river and on the open savanna where the terrain is easier and without as many surprises. To the west is the escarpment of the Muchinga Hills. To the east, over the river, are rolling hills that extend all the way to Malawi.

Moyo and Rumphi are healthy and growing well. They climb over each other and mock charge their elders. Elephants can't jump, but the young ones have a stiff-legged way of bouncing as they learn to run, sometimes tripping and stumbling over their big feet. Moyo has learned to drink with her trunk. Though Rumphi has already grown as big as Moyo, his trunk is still a floppy toy attached to his face which he swings around as he runs. Moyo seems to enjoy being more coordinated than him. She is often the instigator with a headbutt or side push. Mosi continues to be the hill for the two little ones to climb and tumble down. Rumphi is easygoing. He likes to lean on his protectors or to position himself under their back legs and look out from underneath

them. Getting strong and learning how to respond to each other, Moyo and Rumphi will be both powerful and gentle.

When there is more food and water available, other species are not as dependent on elephants and do not follow them. Lua knows this range better than any animal. Every new season, she is aware that humans have cultivated more farmland. She uses her internal map to avoid them, establishing alternate routes to find other increasingly scarce sources of food.

Lua stands and feels the changes around her, evaluating her surroundings for a radius of several miles in every direction. Only her head and trunk move as she bobs her head quietly, searching for a scent. She considers a lifetime of knowledge and memory for places—especially food and water, changing landscapes, and dangers that are old and new—as she plans their day and their weeks ahead.

As Lua considers her family's future, she feels a beating, rhythmic pressure. She calls to the others; they turn and run toward the closest trees, which stand alongside a small bluff. The people in the helicopter know when they encounter elephants who lived through culling operations many years ago. Elephants that remember are quicker to respond, to panic when they feel the whirring of the helicopter with the superpredators inside. The fear is obvious from far above.

The helicopter moves on as the family continues into the trees. Lua waits long after the frightening pulsation is gone. Sumina understands, but the younger elephants have no experience that gives this meaning. Tunya takes it all in; she stands at the edge of the trees looking out, feeling the world around her.

Sensing and integrating information are natural for Tunya, but she is learning how to interpret and use the information. From now on, Tunya will recognize these new sensations and associate them with fear, will know to run for cover. Fear of the loud and unfamiliar is simple. Tunya is also starting to know the complex signals of animals around her, how to recognize when the zebras or impalas alert to lions or humans, or when other elephants, unseen, tell Lua where they have foraged, so she knows the places to avoid. Lua will also teach Tunya how to smell the difference between humans who are predators and those who are not, and how to recognize threat by the distinctive languages they speak. This is more than Tunya can learn from experience. This is why she needs a mother.

LINGUISTS IDENTIFY THE NUMBER OF LANGUAGES *spoken across Africa as anywhere from 1,000 to 3,000. It depends on how you count language groups or whether you consider dialects as separate languages or subsets of a unifying language. Regardless of how they are counted, those languages represent the history of distinct people across the continent, of diverse identities, experience, and life within incredibly unique places. Luangwa Valley, Ituri Forest (the Heart of Darkness), Mt. Kilimanjaro, Namib Desert, Nile River, Mosi-ao-Tunya (Victoria Falls)—are some of the most spectacular geographical sites in the world.*

Elephants used to roam most of Africa. The languages spoken across the continent represent diverse groups of people who spread out and developed cultural identity in places where elephants thrived and shaped the land. This coexistence led to an abundance and variety of traditional lore surrounding elephants or the relationships between elephants and people. There are allegories, such as why the elephant has little eyes—because the tortoise tricked the greedy elephant out of his eyes, and then the elephant stole his new eyes from a worm. In some places, a vengeful neighbor takes the form of an elephant and destroys crops. There was also a man who used magic to make his wife's teeth grow long like an elephant's tusk, then they removed the tusks to sell the ivory. After doing this repeatedly, she turned into an elephant. This story belies the reality that throughout history most Africans did not have much use for ivory, not until Europeans wanted it.

Many cultures hold a mystical reverence for elephants. Their stories may be used to explain the elephant's intelligence and human-like character. There are origin stories for both elephants and humans, in which one turns into the other. Elephant is often a woman. She may go back and forth between her forms by putting on or taking off her elephant skin. She is a wife and perhaps has many elephant descendants. In some places, human leaders or chiefs become elephants when they depart their human lives. It is a sign of respect for elephants and is a testament to the deep connection that people feel with them.

4. *Give and Take*

MAY

The family continues the spreading of seeds over long distances in the coming weeks. As the rains temper and cease, the elephants turn north. The land bakes quickly, leaving their footprints as rough pockmarks in the soil. Or, as author and Colonial District Officer Kenneth Bradley imagined it, a stout woman sat down and shaped the ground underneath her.

Lua wants to be close to the river in the land that is most familiar when the dry season peaks. She must know the land well for her family to live and to thrive, especially at that time of year. They will travel hundreds of miles through the valley, arriving at their dry season home as the air heats up and the lush green begins to turn brown.

Moyo has been eating bits of food that Lua or Tunya drop. She still cannot control her trunk well enough to eat on her own, so she picks up dropped leaves or shoots with her mouth and flops her little trunk out of the way to protect it. Soon Moyo will imitate her mother, clumsily copying Lua's coordinated minuet of twisting her trunk around stems, delicately pulling up plants, shaking or kicking dirt from the roots, and then placing the plant in her mouth. Today Moyo watched Lua strip shoots from a branch and scratch her leg with it. With great concentration, Moyo picked up a stick and flailed it around briefly before she dropped it and went to push on Tunya.

Before long, Moyo's trunk will be her primary way to explore the world close around her. Elephants can't hide their curiosity when their attention is focused at the end of their trunks. The nose-in-hand reaches out to investigate its space. Instead of bringing an object to her nose, Lua moves her nose to the object.

Lua's eyes are far to the side of her head, marking her as prey not predator. Standing before you, she would have to raise her head and look down or cock her head to the side to see you. But she wouldn't do either of those things. She might start with a trunk tip in your face with the sensitive nerve endings discovering your state of being, your level of fear—given away by your hormones or the sweat she detects from your forehead or your armpits.

There's not much that you can hide from a curious elephant. When Lua touches your chest, she feels your heartbeat and breath. If she feels distress, her nose-in-hand organ could become her assess-and-comfort organ. She may lay her trunk over your shoulder and rumble a low, calming reassurance.

Assessing and comforting is one of Lua's most important jobs as leader of the family. Her role is about much more than finding food and water, it is also about well-being. Because elephants never forget, they carry all of their experiences with them. The effects of distress and family disruption can leave behind the aftermath of trauma for decades.

Over the next few months, the family settles into a pattern of movement with daily excursions that overlap but slowly shift north. Elephants and humans of the region feel that the dry season seems earlier and warmer than the last. And as humans continue to expand their range, there's greater competition for food in the elephants' ever-smaller areas and less time for plants to regrow. Overly grazed plants with extra heat and little water are a disaster for wildlife and humans.

Every year, the lives of Stary and Mulenga revolve around the seasons in a cycle that has become a spiral. In the past, sometimes early in the morning at the beginning of the cold season in May, Mulenga would see ice at the edge of the *dambo*, the shallow wetlands left over from the rains. There hasn't been ice in many years, and the land suffers between drought and flood, neither of which support life in a place where crops are exclusively rainfed.

When lack of water kills plants, erosion increases, contributing to floods, and destroying more plants. It's a paradox that too little water leads to unpredictable floods. Hydropower accounts for more than 80 percent of electricity production in this part of the world. If the water dries up due to heat and vegetation loss, there's no electricity. Stary has started working with an organization that is planting vetiver or elephant grasses along the waterways to reduce erosion, to keep the land and its nutrients intact. In places that flood, they are building channels to allow the water to escape. People like Stary and Mulenga contribute almost nothing to climate change but feel its effects the most.

Mulenga knows that if the average temperature continues to rise, the maize will not flower at all, and the primary food source for her family and all Zambians will fail. She doesn't know the exact temperature that is too high, but she knows that the rise is because of people in faraway places. She doesn't understand their lives, and they don't understand hers.

AS THE DRY SEASON STRETCHES AHEAD, Lua and her family settle in close to the river, as much as elephants ever settle. They forage in the early morning and late evening with a drink after each, taking a shady rest during the middle of the day when the sun is at its most unforgiving.

This morning the family moves to a mopane thicket in the western portion of the park. They bypass the mopane that burned at the peak of the dry season more than a year ago, an agricultural fire that got out of hand. The fire burned too hot without enough rain afterword to be a regenerative fire. The mopane lost its canopy, and the grasses have not returned.

The little ones don't play much in the heat, and the adults walk slowly, saving energy. By late morning, they reach the western thicket and browse. It's early in the dry season and the trees have recovered from when the family passed this spot on their way south a few months ago. Lua's mental navigational map includes spatiotemporal relationships that she uses to plan for this time of year, knowing that the trees will have rebounded enough to support her family again as they move north. Her large home range—and leaving the trees for a period of recovery—is vital to their survival.

The mopane tree prevails throughout Southern Africa in the low-lying regions with little rainfall and high heat. Many factors influence the range and health of mopane, including altitude, fire, soil suitability, animals who eat it, and humans who use it for wood or charcoal. Mopane grows efficiently and is more drought tolerant than many tree species. It can also undermine other plants by sending out chemicals into the soil that prevent nearby growth of other trees or grasses, creating isolated stands of mopane without many verdant interlopers.

Though monocultural plant growth can have its problems, mopane is essential to life in these areas. In classic coevolutionary fashion, when animals browse on the mopane tree, especially during the growth stage, the tree releases phenol-based compounds, such as tannins found in wine, into its shoots and leaves. These defense chemicals make the tree taste bad to many species, including elephants. So, Lua and family only eat a little and then move on. This effectively makes elephants good pruners, thinning out small branches so that the ones left behind can grow longer and produce larger leaves the next year.

By browsing this site early in the growing season, Lua and family stimulated the trees to regrow their leaves before the worst of the dry season and to hold onto their leaves later in the year than other trees. Even though she only eats other parts of the tree at this point in the season, other animals eat the leaves. Stary brings his goats here and other men in the village bring their cattle. Mopane leaves have high protein content, helping animals to fortify their diets when not much else is available.

After eating, Lua chooses a short route to the closest water hole in the opposite direction that she ultimately wants to go for the day, back toward the river. They are more than half a mile away when Lua hears men's voices and the sounds of their goats drinking.

This area is a low point of the river basin and endemic with sleeping sickness. Humans moved from this place many generations ago, leaving the land for 100 square miles to be governed by elephants and buffalo. Livestock herders don't usually come here for fear of disease in themselves and their animals. But they risk it because their usual sources are dry, and they are struggling to find water. Lua recognizes their patterns of speech and their familiar, fearsome scent. She can tell they are young, but adults. She quietly turns and the family runs in silence farther away from the river to the closest water hole.

The elephants are overheated by the time they get to the next water hole which is drier and muddier than elephants can drink. They may have to look for shade and wait until the day cools before moving back in the direction of the river. Moyo walks into the water to lay down. Tunya follows her and helps Moyo climb out, but Tunya's weight has caused her to sink deep into the mud and her feet are stuck. Lua paces on the bank, rumbling back and forth with Tunya. Her normal calm and collected demeanor gets rattled, and she finally wades in to try to help extricate Tunya from the mud. Lua is stronger, but she also weighs more. She also gets stuck.

The family is in distress but does not follow Tunya and Lua into the mud. Sumina watches, helpless, on the water's edge. Minutes pass into hours. Sumina keeps the family close for the rest of the day and night. The morning is no better with the two elephants still mired in the mud. The more they struggle to get out, the more they seem to be stuck. Sumina nervously leads Rumphi and Mosi back to the mopane thicket. Moyo stays with her mother and sister, waiting next to the quagmire.

Other animals come and go from the water hole. Some animals will drink dirty water that the elephants will not. Lua and Tunya stand there and watch as life continues around them. This is the first time that Lua has been unable to help Tunya. Moyo is laying down by the water's edge and not moving much. A lion or even a pack of hyenas could find her right now and there is nothing that Lua could do.

Days and nights are close to equal here. Every day receives twelve hours of radiant sun. The sidereal day takes the same amount of time at every point on the earth, no matter the latitude or the circumference of the earth at any precise location. In other words, a revolution takes 24 hours regardless of the distance traveled. If Lua was stuck at the north pole, she would be spinning on the planet's surface at less than a meter per hour. Here the world spins at almost 1,000 miles an hour. Sunrise and sunset are fast, a few minutes of brilliant blue and orange twice a day, but it feels like an eternity as the earth rotates, turning so quickly as Lua is motionless. She can do nothing but stand and wait as time moves on.

Night falls as Lua revolves underneath the unmoving stars. Some of these stars have already collapsed in on themselves with a violent burst of energy—their brightness cast many light-years ago and only reaching her now after their spark has gone out.

By morning the elephants are exhausted. Lua feels the vibration of a motorcycle coming toward them. She doesn't know what this portends but knows she and her daughters won't last much longer. On the motorcycle, Stary is searching for an adventurous goat who disappeared during the night. He sees the elephants standing motionless in the water and recognizes immediately they are in trouble.

Stary parks close to the water hole and gets out for a look. Only then he realizes that the gray bump on the water's edge is a little elephant. From his manner and scent, Lua believes Stary isn't dangerous. He moves to the opposite side of the water from Moyo to avoid further distressing the elephants. He can feel the shudder in the air from Lua's calls to Tunya and Moyo, though he can't hear it. Moyo doesn't rise or react. Stary can't tell if the little one is alive. He stands and looks at the elephants for several minutes and then drives away.

He returns with Mwamba, a friend. The two men approach cautiously. This time, Moyo moves her head slightly and they know she is alive. Stary and Mwamba unload a trough of water from the truck. They hope that Moyo will get up and drink, but she doesn't. The men consider the elephants and discuss what to do. They decide they'll have to get within reach of the elephants' trunks and tusks, either of which can be deadly. They test the elephants by getting closer; Tunya and Lua don't react. With some reassurance from Lua, Tunya accepts the men are trying to help.

Carefully, Stary and Mwamba get on either side of Tunya. Stary throws long straps to Mwamba, and they ease the straps behind her and attach them to the back of the truck. Stary slowly guides the truck forward while Mwamba watches Tunya and yells to Stary. Tunya's back feet move up and out of the suction of the mud, but her front feet are still stuck. They reposition the straps and include her front legs this time.

Again, Stary moves the truck forward, and now Tunya's body shifts as her front feet are released from the mud. The truck and the straps slowly pull her forward until she can climb out. The men cheer, and clap each other on the back.

Tunya is weak and shaky. She should get a drink, but instead she walks to Moyo and then turns to watch as the men figure out how to help her mother. There's no guidebook for pulling elephants out of mud. The men must move farther into the water to get to Lua.

The men position the straps and Stary pulls himself through the mud past Lua. He climbs out of the mud and into the truck. Eventually, the men are able to ease Lua up and onto the bank. She steps away from the straps and over to her daughters.

The men move the truck off to the side and sit on the tailgate to watch the elephants recover. The dry air can't wick the sweat away as the men sit after their effort in the spiteful sun. Sweat trickles down the back of Stary's neck and his legs. It feels as though they are inside of a stove, but they don't care.

The three elephants, barely clinging to life, are safe for the moment. Lua and Tunya take a long drink from the trough that the men have offered. The water is clean and cool. Lua puts water into Moyo's mouth and tries to get her to stand. It will still be a challenge to get back to the river, but they have no choice other than to move on. The men watch as the three elephants walk slowly and silently into the distance. Dusk descends, and the trio becomes dark shapes against the backdrop of a spectacular pink sky.

Today at the water hole Stary didn't have to compete with the elephants for water or food. He feels a satisfaction from helping them that he has not felt since his children were small and needed him more.

As Lua and her daughters move back toward the river and their family, Lua begins to call to Sumina, the reluctant leader in Lua's absence. Lua stops again at the mopane thicket. She must eat or she'll have no milk for Moyo. Moyo is too tired to eat the scraps that the others drop. She lies down and does not want to get up again. Lua allows her little one to nap while she and Tunya eat, but finally they help Moyo up so that she can nurse.

While Moyo nurses, Lua triangulates her position in the valley. She smells and feels the land, and her place in it. She needs to find the shortest distance to the river and determine relative benefits and risks of departing from the course for food or water along the way. They may not survive another mistake.

By evening Lua makes contact with Sumina. They feel each other through the ground and start moving toward each other. As the family reunites there is great trumpeting and general excitement, especially from Sumina, who did not go without food or water for days. Lua realizes that Mosi is not there. While his mother was trapped, he left with a group of males.

The next day Stary rents a water truck and returns to the dry water hole to fill it. He will do this twice a week when the earth is scorched, and the animals have no water. He knows the earth is warming. He knows the water is lower every year and that it gets contaminated by too many animals using water that is barely more than a mud puddle. He can't fill all the water holes, but he can fill that one.

NO MATTER HOW MANY NUTRIENTS *the soil gets from elephants, plants can't grow without water. Elephants were once blamed for the loss of acacia trees and subsequent desertification of the Serengeti in Tanzania. In response, some of the elephants were culled. Later evidence showed that the desertification was due to the human activity of burning overgrown pastures. When elephants recovered in the area so did the acacia trees.*

Similarly, during a period of severe drought in the 1970s in Kenya, loss of plants was attributed to elephants. At the time, there was a public request for assistance in providing the elephants with water. The appeal used the slogan, "Buy an elephant a drink." One man, a Kenyan of British descent who had a business of culling and ivory trading in the latter part of the 20th century, claimed there were simply too many elephants in the area, and some needed to be killed to avoid irreversible loss of plant life. Instead of giving them a drink, he argued for, "Buy an elephant a bullet."

On the surface it seems logical; elephants were eating the plants, and the plants were dying. There was a great debate about culling at the time, and ultimately it did not happen. After the drought was over, the plants returned even though the elephants remained.

Researcher Iain Douglas-Hamilton wrote that, "With the rains came an amazing and totally unexpected regeneration of acacias which flourished despite the high numbers of elephants. This seemed to fly in the face of several theories about elephants and trees, all of which argued that a high elephant density completely suppressed regeneration."

5. *Elephants and Humans*

OCTOBER

Mosi travels with the males now. He is the smallest and youngest by a couple of years. None of them are strangers. Some he played with when their families socialized. Some are probably related to him through his father. They may know this or not, but during Mosi's lifetime he will likely choose companions who are kin—one of the mysteries of elephant life. Maybe they can smell it with those sensitive noses or taste it when they gently touch each other's mouths.

Without babies in tow, this group moves faster than his mother. They are bolder but not more organized. As long as these males stay healthy, they are not targets for predators other than humans. Mosi's tusks are coming in, those beautiful long teeth, set deep into his jaw—the downfall of elephants everywhere. Right now, Mosi is mostly an observer, a follower. He's learning the ways of the bull. He will learn routes that his mother never uses; the little ones can't cross deep rivers or travel as far. Lua also gives humans an extra wide berth unless she is certain they aren't a threat.

Bulls live in hierarchy of status with older bulls at the top. Since they grow throughout most of their lives, the oldest are usually the biggest and most powerful. Mosi will need to learn their social rules to form a group and survive his youth. He has smelled the scent of the old bulls when they are seeking his mother or aunties, and even tried a play version of mounting in imitation of the movements. But Mosi does not understand the feeling of massive amounts of testosterone coursing through his body like they do. Unless the old bulls in this area are killed, Mosi won't likely experience the raging testosterone of musth until well into his twenties.

Mosi and his new companions, other adolescent males, stay close to some older bulls. They interact at the water hole and in passing. Like the other young bulls, Mosi greets his older counterparts by touching their mouths with the tip of his trunk.

As the day heats up, he and three young bulls wander to the river. They plunge into the water, spray each other, wrap trunks, and trumpet. This never gets old for elephants. They push each other in a playful show of strength. Mosi lays down with his left side in the water and his trunk in the air, relaxing and enjoying himself. His right feet kick up and out of the water, so that only the bottoms of his feet and the tip of his trunk are visible.

Elephants run hot. Any large animal retains heat, with a small ratio of skin to body size. Mosi must maintain a low metabolism with a normal heart rate of thirty beats per minute and a normal respiratory rate as low as four breaths per minute. The big veins that spread across the surface of his ears also help him regulate his temperature. When he flaps the massive pinnae, it cools the blood inside the veins by several degrees, lowering his body heat. Even the wiry hairs loosely scattered across his cracked skin provide heat release. Perhaps young elephants like Moyo and Rumphi are extra fuzzy with hair because their other heat dissipation mechanisms aren't fully developed.

Water is vital for keeping Mosi cool, and not only the water he drinks. His skin is as dry and cracked as it appears, with no sweat glands or oil glands. The fissures are deep and sharp enough to cut tender human skin just by running a hand along the underside of his trunk. The crevices increase the surface area of his skin for passive cooling. The rough surface also allows the movement and storage of water across the surface of his body. On smooth skin, water runs off. On sculptured elephant skin, water is like surface irrigation for rows of crops. Water flows into the channels and molecular tension keeps it in place.

Elephants, rhinos, and hippos are somewhat unique within the animal kingdom, other than humans, with exposed skin and little hair. Hippo skin doesn't have cracks like elephants' but does have regular shallow grooves. Hippos also lack sweat or oil glands, but they secrete a mucous-like substance onto the skin which helps store water. Besides this physiologic adaptation to the heat of the African savanna, hippos stay in the water during the day and forage on land at night, a behavioral adaptation. Rhinos vary a lot by species, but African rhinos do have sweat glands. Though they look like living tanks and have a thick hide, their epidermis is thin. Their heat adaptation is both sweat and passive release through the thin stratum corneum.

The elephants of Namibia, the dryland to the west, are also African savanna elephants but have earned themselves the title of *desert elephants*. Known for their leggy appearance, their height is an illusion due to their smaller bodies connected to legs of the same length as other savanna elephants. Smaller bodies are an adaptation to living with minimal water and food. Their feet are wider so that they don't sink into the sandy soil as they walk close to 100 miles a day to find the sustenance they need. These elephants also live in smaller family groups, a cultural difference developed in response to resources.

The variation in elephant populations across Africa—both physiologic and behavioral adaptations developed over millennia—tell a story of the effects of isolation and environment on a species. But for all elephants, the key to living in challenging surroundings across a vast landscape is an impeccable memory of where the water and food are, and the intelligence to know how those resources are affected by prevailing conditions of rainfall and heat or the activity of human animals. Survival is dependent on understanding and adjusting.

Perhaps Mosi knows this as he delights in the water. Perhaps he plays as if his life depends on it.

Mosi emerges from the river with a thin layer of water that makes a delicate membrane along the deep crevices of his skin. If he then covers that layer with dirt, he creates mud that will retain water to his underlying skin for more than a day. Wallowing in mud has the same effect. Even when he stands in the dry sun and throws dirt over himself, he is preventing evaporative losses which helps keep him cool. The color of the dirt on Mosi's skin tells the story of where he's been.

As Mosi follows the group away from the river he becomes aware of his mother's voice. She has been calling to him since they were separated days ago, and now he responds. He runs to her, and she greets him with throaty calls and touches. Though he has been learning to be a stoic elephant bull, his joy is visible as he lays down and Moyo and Rumphi climb on top of him. He didn't know that his mother and sisters were alive. Though he has returned to his family for now, he will start spending a day or two with the bulls when they are near. Eventually, he will leave his mother and family.

Lua is extra careful, knowing that Moyo was very near death at the water hole, with Tunya and herself not far behind. Life slowly returns to normal, the normal daily challenges of being an elephant in a part of the world on the brink of being unlivable for either animals or people. Scientists are studying what temperatures are incompatible with life, and the physiologic changes that occur inside a body that slowly bakes over years, such as increased stress on the heart, kidneys, and even changes in blood flow to the brain. Will the heat itself kill, or will lack of food and water do it first?

At this point in the dry season, the elephants are again followed by other animals, the nyala and impala. Lua is nervous to move her family away from the river and the shallow pools nearby, but they need to eat. Moyo, the self-assured daughter of the family leader surrounded by loving elders—her feistiness is tempered by hunger. The babies are at risk of not growing and thriving.

Meanwhile Stary forms a habit around delivering water to the animals. He empties the truck and then sits on the tailgate, waits, and watches as the animals come to drink. Lua learns the sound of the truck. She recognizes the significance of the vibrations and returns to the water hole which had been the site of danger. As Lua begins to anticipate his arrival, the family browses in nearby trees until she feels the waves of gushing water filling the muddy pool. Then the elephants move into sight, reminding Stary of the old legends of elephants mysteriously appearing out of nowhere, just at the right moment.

By the end of the season, Lua knows his schedule and does not need to wait in the nearby trees. They simply show up when he is there. They meet at the water hole on a regular basis. Stary fills with happiness, knowing that the elephants have become used to his presence. He also understands he can't stop bringing the water until the rains fall again. Sometimes after they drink, the elephants move toward Stary and simply stand for several minutes facing him before they walk away and across the horizon. Moyo once charged him with her ears out, making a squeaky little trumpet sound, but Tunya came and got her and guided her back to the family.

Stary is grateful that his wife, Mulenga, is easy to get along with and teaches their children about plants. Usually quiet, when she laughs, everyone laughs. Mulenga is the grandchild of a man who went to an illegal school run by African men during colonial days. Back then this land was still called Northern Rhodesia. In addition to their traditional school lessons, the students were taught about colonialism and its converse, national independence. Mulenga's great-grandmother insisted that her son be educated, though the illegal school was eventually closed, and her grandfather received a beating by colonial police.

Mulenga comes from a long line of strong women, as she is herself. She and four other women of her village applied for a micro-loan to increase their ways to earn money. She and Stary used the loan to build a solar powered water pump on their land. The well only provides enough water for their household use, but it makes Mulenga's life simpler. She has more time to spend doing other things like collecting plants or fruits from the forest which Stary can take to the city market. She also knows how to make medicines and salves from what she finds. Their children are rarely sick.

The five women applied for a loan as a unit. Mulenga received the first loan and repaid it after a year with interest; then the loan was made under the same terms to the second member of the group. They share the obligation to repay the loan, but each one will support the others as they work to make money during the year. As individuals, they feel a commitment to cover their own loans because if they default, next year's installment will not come in from the bank for the next member of the group.

LUA IS HOPING TO OUTLAST THE DRY SEASON without having to move the family, but then overnight she hears gunshots from the west. Hunters have started moving into the edge of the park at night, coming over the escarpment. This happens more when the crops fail, and when poverty is high. They are mostly hunting for bush meat, such as impala or bushbuck, though they will take what they can get. The elephants move toward the eastern edge of the park.

Gunshots become a regular occurrence over the next few weeks. Food is dwindling, and the elephants need to move to find the few grasses that are edible at this time of year. Like the mopane tree, savanna grasses evolved along with elephants and other large herbivores. They are specially adapted to regrow after periods of heavy grazing, but they need enough time for that to happen.

Late one morning, as the family is browsing, a small group of elephants moves slowly toward them. Mosi is curious and the only one to investigate. The group consists of two barely adolescent females and a male, the young remnants of a family whose mothers were killed by hunters. They are scared, thirsty, and hungry. Lua's family is struggling, and now they have a ragtag group of orphans in tow. The new arrivals are not welcomed.

It would be different if resources were abundant. If Lua accepted the orphans into the family, it would add to her burden of finding food and water. Right now, they have no extra to share. The orphans follow the family at a distance, relying on Lua for her knowledge of relative safety and hoping to find sustenance, but not for comfort.

The orphans are the right age to be good playmates for Mosi, but they don't play. Mosi tries to engage the younger bull. He crouches on his front legs like a dog or pushes the newcomer head-on, but the young bull simply turns away. The females also show no interest. They relive the terror of losing their mothers and can't pay much attention to anything else.

It's now early December, the end of the dry season, and the air is hot, but as the sun sets quickly, the breeze picks up and cools the air. Lua senses distant rain and the family starts moving toward it. It will take some time for their fodder to rebound, but at least it's not as hot, and they will find water. Also, the rainy season makes it harder for humans to move in and out of the areas where elephants can go. Maybe they will get relief from that too.

They have all survived another cycle of seasons, but they can't know if the lives of the little ones have been shortened by the stress of the last few weeks. When every year is a struggle for survival, will the young elephants of today ever be as healthy as their ancestors? Has their DNA been altered in a way that they will not be able to withstand the challenges to come?

The old bull of the area spends an afternoon near the family. His odor of musth signaled his arrival long before he was visible to Lua. She doesn't pay the big bull much obvious attention. None of the females are in estrus. Tunya could be of age. Occasionally, females bear children by the age of twelve, but many will not until late in their teen years. It is possible that none of them will go into estrus while they are so stressed from heat, hunger, thirst, and fear. The old bull checks each female for signs of readiness, then moves on. His entourage of younger males is not far off, and Mosi leaves with them. He does not know that it is the last time he will see Tunya.

ONE WINDY AFTERNOON, THE FAMILY IS GRAZING in open grass and Lua does not hear or feel the vibration of the trucks until they are close. They are moving fast. Lua alerts the others, but there is no time to respond before she recognizes that terrifying pulsation through the air. Lua runs as fast as the little ones can go, but the helicopter swings around and approaches them from the front. The family is in disarray.

The two female orphans are already apart from the group and easy to distance from the others. The men hit each with a tranquilizer dart, then come after Tunya, trying to separate her from the herd. She panics and runs, but she is also darted and crumples forward. One of her tusks breaks with a thunderous, splintering crack as she hits the ground.

Lua sees Tunya fall and turns back while Sumina and the boys continue to run. With Moyo following, Lua rushes to Tunya's side and tries to lift her with her tusks. The helicopter attempts to scare Lua away, but she doesn't budge. Finally, the men shoot Lua with a tranquilizer dart. She fights the sedative for a minute but then falls hard. Trucks and men quickly surround the elephants. Moyo frantically tries to protect her mother, but the men aren't after Lua.

They get into position and use a crane to lift Tunya and the other two young females into a truck. After the three elephants are loaded, the men scare Moyo away and then use a truck to keep her at bay. They give Lua an injection that will reverse the sedative and leave in a rush. Moyo is there, pushing desperately at Lua, trying to wake her. Moyo feels her mother's breathing and heartbeat with her fleshy feet. She has seen Sumina do this with Rumphi in her way of motherly assessment, but Moyo does not know how to interpret what she feels.

Lua wakes up bewildered and groggy, and eventually stands. She calls for Tunya but gets no answer. In a daze she begins to look for her daughter. Moyo follows as closely as she can. Lua searches by calling, then listens by feeling the air for a response. She raises her trunk and smells many unfamiliar and scary scents lingering in the air. Tunya's scent tells a story of an elephant who was there and now is gone.

OUR TRADITIONAL, FLAT WAY OF LOOKING AT THE EARTH *on a map causes visual distortions, especially of land masses near the poles compared to those of the equator. The illusion created by flattening out the globe makes it look like Canada and Russia make up about twenty-five percent of the earth's surface, but these countries are only about five percent. The equator runs through the heart of Africa, at the maximal circumference around the earth. In fact, earth's rotation causes it to bulge at the equator, further warping our understanding of the true size of the continent, which is larger than India, China, the mainland US, and most of Europe all put together.*

It is difficult to comprehend the remoteness of the places where elephants live, which is not to say that there are no people there. All over the world, people live in remote places with animals. The skill of this cohabitation is largely dependent on how long it has been going on. These are areas often isolated by difficult terrain, endemic disease or pests, harsh climates, and almost invariably by poverty.

One of the reasons that elephants remained in specific regions of Africa is their ability to coexist with the tsetse fly, which carries the parasite that causes the deadly African sleeping sickness in humans and nagana in cattle. These areas where humans couldn't live or keep cattle remained safe for wildlife.

Sleeping sickness is one of several Neglected Tropical Diseases (NTDs), a term which refers to viral, bacterial, and parasitic infections that mostly afflict portions of Africa, Southeast Asia, and South America. The word "neglected" points out the fact that these diseases, though they cause "devastating health, social, and economic consequences" to more than a billion people worldwide, are largely overlooked compared to diseases that affect more affluent countries. These neglected diseases are preventable or treatable, but poor people and poor countries can't pay the price, contributing to a cycle of poverty.

Combined with demand for wildlife products from wealthier places, poverty motivates wildlife trade, both legal and illegal, in many of these isolated areas. From the outside, it can be hard to understand why people would hunt an animal to extinction, or why it is so difficult for law enforcement to stop illegal hunting. These activities happen in remote areas within a colossal amount of space. The world is big, and life is hard.

The conditions of poverty lead people to believe that we must choose between animals and humans, that there isn't enough space or resources for both, rather than recognizing the multispecies dependencies to which humans belong. Protection of animals, conservation, and human health and development are inextricably linked. Trying to treat them as separate issues doesn't work—a healthy ecosystem that supports animal life is also the best to support human life. When wild animals lose space and habitat, contact and conflict with humans increase. Taking care of the needs of wild animals can help keep people safe and increase the success of coexistence. Reduction of poverty also decreases reliance on wildlife as resources for food or income.

Entomologist and author Edward Wilson compared clearing land where endangered animals live to burning a Renaissance painting to cook dinner. When you are starving and have no other fuel, you will burn the painting. Or as Stephen Matthews quoted one of his African colleagues, "You see a big bird of Africa in all its glory, so you watch and praise Africa for its abundant wildlife. But the poor [man] with a starving family to feed and no money only looks for the best way to trap and kill the bird. Even if it is the only bird left in the whole wide world, so he can feed his dying children—that is the real difference between us."

6. *Moving On*

DECEMBER

The helicopter and trucks have gone, but Lua is disoriented with no way to understand what happened. The family is in disarray. Sumina finds her way back to Lua who is searching for Tunya. Lua calls out for Tunya while crossing the landscape as Moyo struggles after her.

Over the next several days, Lua and Sumina stay in loose contact. As Lua starts to give up her search, she falls into grief. Her cortisol, a stress hormone, is extremely high and reflected in her hyperarousal. She cannot rest, though now she only calls for Tunya a few times a day. Sumina is once again the reluctant leader of the family, not a role she wanted or planned for. Her own formative years were disrupted with the death of her mother, so she didn't learn how to organize a family and navigate in their interests, as Tunya was learning from Lua.

In her grief, Lua follows Sumina. Sumina applies mud to Lua's open sore from the tranquilizer dart and holds it closed with her trunk fingers until the mud dries. This helps stop the bleeding and allows a scab to form.

The young male orphan stays on the edge of the family and hardly eats, his distress hovering in the air. The other elephants sense it. One evening Rumphi approaches the orphan and touches his trunk and face. The older male places his trunk on Rumphi's head as they briefly walk side by side.

The family fumbles through the next few days which stretch into weeks. Tunya's removal and Lua's listless demeanor have left the others scared and confused. Elephants understand death but not helicopters and tranquilizer guns or the disappearance of one of their own. The change in his mother and family triggers Mosi to move on with the bull group.

The bulls heard the helicopter too. Like Lua and Sumina, the old bulls remember this sound from their youth. That sound has only ever meant trouble, and they are wary, but this time the helicopter was not for them.

Tunya and six other young female elephants are on board a Boeing 747, headed to the United States. After several weeks of observation and veterinary checkups, they were each deemed healthy enough to travel and unlikely to carry disease. The group of seven has been moved into specially built cages and given mild sedatives for the flight, but these are animals built for the expanses of Africa, a slow life built around scent, sound, and touch. Tunya's body amplifies every vibration.

The two orphans taken with Tunya have retreated into themselves and into each other. The sisters are in constant contact, but, like the others, are barely eating. Their temporary caretakers are hoping this will get better when they settle into a stable new home.

MOSI AND THE BULLS MOVE IN A LOOSE GROUP, not like the formation of his maternal family. The old bulls are nearby, sometimes visible, often not. The young bulls do not let them get too far away.

As the smallest bull, Mosi is carefully deferential to his elders. For his whole life he has been the grandson or son of the family leader, and his needs have always been important within the family. Now he must learn life without his mother. The bigger he gets, the more he is capable of being destructive and unwelcome by humans or other animals. Learning the ways of a proper elephant bull is vital.

Mosi finds an older bull, Yama, who tolerates his presence. Perhaps Yama is an uncle or cousin, or simply a gentle giant. He allows Mosi to follow closely when he is eating or at the water hole. He lets Mosi stand in his shade when the sun is unrelenting. Sometimes Mosi takes a nap and leans on the big bull. Yama shows Mosi his favorite foraging spots and leads him to a protected corridor that connects wildlife from the western part of Southern Africa to the floodplains of the Zambezi, a vital link of populations and genetics. One night as they pass a tourist lodge, Yama picks up some garbage on the ground and puts it in the bin nearby.

Yama does not yet qualify as an old bull, but at the age of twenty-eight, he is getting close. Over the last few years, he has had short periods of heightened testosterone, but the presence of the truly old bulls has prevented his full musth—a social-physiological phenomenon. Yama has never successfully mated; usually this does not happen until the age of thirty-five or more. Such is the reality of this long-lived animal.

As the two elephants walk to the water hole together, Mosi moves off to the side while Yama approaches the region's dominant male. As Mosi steps to the edge of the water and starts to drink, the two older bulls signal each other. They stand face-to-face in apparent silence for several minutes, sharing cues only they appreciate. Finally, Yama approaches the grand bull and places the tip of his trunk in the older one's mouth. As the old bull slowly backs up, Mosi greets him too. When their ritual is complete, the big bull turns from the water hole and moves off into the distance. Mosi steps toward Yama and stands beside his protector while Yama takes a long drink.

Because of Yama, Mosi is no longer on the fringe of the group, though he must still be aware of his place among them as the little newcomer. They travel freely, following distant rain and stopping to forage along the way. They can go for longer without water than Lua and the young.

By January, rain fills the parched, cracked land. Trees turn green and fresh shoots appear overnight. The sharp, sweet smell of cut grass fills the air when they eat. The bulls are making the most of the rains. Though still young to be away from his mother's family, Mosi benefits from the rich food that the bulls can find by traveling farther than Lua can. They are eating and playing their way across the savanna, pushing, and throwing grass at each other, an elephant celebration of abundance.

A few months pass as the bulls enjoy the rainy season. Yama is well-fed and healthy. His testosterone levels begin to surge, his first full musth, and he must go look for a mate. His mission starts out as a wander toward the areas where families are more likely to be. He vocalizes some long calls, hoping to hear an estrus call in response. Elephant cows may only be in estrus for two to six days every four to six years, so breeding pairs must be able to find each other over vast distances at the right time. Yama needs to be efficient in his search.

After several days on the move, he feels a response to his call. His movements now have a target, and he walks more pointedly toward this female with his silent, grand strides. Yama is now in the full throes of musth, with secretions streaming from his temporal glands and his penis releasing both urine and a strong odor that advertises his status. His testosterone levels are more than ten times normal, and he has only one thing on his mind.

Yama is exceptional at localizing sound, knowing his surroundings and where things are in space without detailed vision. For any animal, unless the source of a noise is exactly equally distant from both ears, each ear receives the sound waves at a momentary difference in time. The brain automatically compares the time difference, which enables sound localization. Yama is so good at this partly due to the size of his head. The time gap between his ears is greater than any other land animal which provides additional information for more precise localization.

Yama's ears are far apart, but his feet are much farther, and he can use the vibrations in his feet to triangulate position in addition to the information from his ears. Very low frequency sounds, such as their mating calls received through the ground, would be difficult to recognize with a smaller detection system than the distance between his feet. Acoustic waves and seismic waves also have different rates of transmission and decay, meaning that he can likely compare the temporal information from his ears and feet for more precise clues to the location of a sound. Yama is built for finding a mate over a great distance.

As he nears the family group, Yama's nose takes over and he finds his estrus female by scent. She would prefer an older male and avoids Yama. He follows her for two days and repeatedly approaches her, but she runs away from him. On the third day, the grand bull of the region arrives, and Yama has to make a choice: fight a bigger bull or give up. Perhaps if he can displace the old bull—two 13,000-pound animals battling each other head-on—he can convince the female of his suitability. But Yama knows his limits and chooses to yield.

The appearance of the old bull and the loss of his target of interest spur Yama to move on. As time passes and his testosterone levels go down, he heads back to find Mosi and his group of bachelors.

Without Yama, the group of adolescents is more disorganized and not as careful. Yama understands risk better than the younger bulls, but in his testosterone-induced turmoil, he left them too close to a village. They smell maize, which has more calories than their normal fodder and can help them grow strong. But stealing from a farmer is asking for trouble.

The young bulls are usually not bold enough to seek out cultivated food but the sweet scent of ripening maize drifts in the clear evening air. They are too tempted to turn down the special treat—opportunism rather than a plan. Mosi moves nervously through the field. He explores something strange in his path and feels a sudden searing, ripping pain

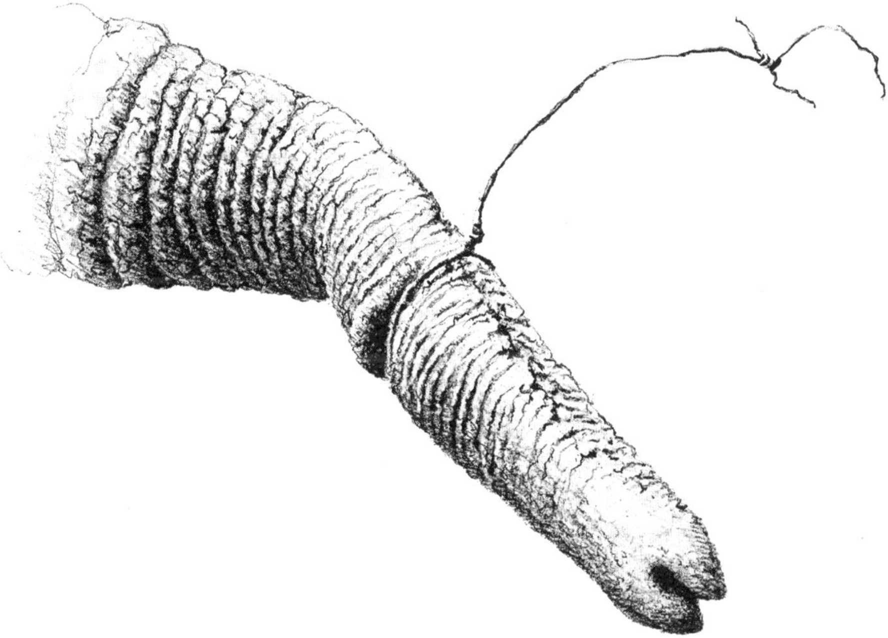

in his trunk. The farmer has set up traps for bush hogs. Mosi panics but the more he tries to pull away, the more the snare cuts into his trunk.

The farmer has become aware of intruders in the field and reacts by rattling cans and shouting. The elephants make a break for it and Mosi has no choice but to run with the snare on his trunk. He struggles to keep up, but the group slows down when they are far enough away from the village. The wire dangles from Mosi's damaged trunk.

Without the use of his trunk, Mosi's connection with the world is muted. Not only does he have trouble eating and drinking, but his vocalizations are also limited. He can smell but can't gather scent, can't explore his surroundings. His greatest strength turned into his greatest weakness.

For the next few days, Mosi follows the group. They carefully put water and food into his mouth, but it is not enough. He gets weaker and weaker. The group slows down to stay with him, but there is not much else they can do to help. Late one morning, they stop at a water hole, and Mosi becomes aware of Yama. Before Yama is visible, his scent travels downwind to Mosi, a silent herald. No longer in musth, Yama has been looking for the group by following them slowly and deliberately. He knows his companions by the scent of each one's urine, though he has not smelled Mosi's for several days.

As Yama gets closer, he understands why he can smell Mosi's blood. The two elephants stand together at the water hole as the other young bulls move away into the distance. Yama and Mosi are so still and silent that they might be mistaken for statues except that the snare moves slightly with the breeze, pulling on Mosi's trunk. Yama considers what to do. Finally, he calls for Mosi to follow him and the two bulls walk together in a new direction. Yama would usually avoid tourists, but he also knows that there are people in the busy part of the park who can help. The two elephants sense the small trucks as they approach. Then they hear voices. Being close to people strikes a new fear in Mosi. This is risky, but he trusts Yama and continues.

In the distance, people with binoculars and radios spot the pair of elephants stepping out of a stand of trees. The humans have not realized that one is in trouble, but they are still mesmerized by the pair moving directly toward them. Yama stops and makes encouraging rumbles to Mosi, who hesitantly continues toward the people. When Mosi gets close enough, the people see the snare on his trunk. He hears the excitement in their voices and then the squawk of a radio. He simply stands there until two other vehicles arrive. The drivers get out and talk while they look at Mosi, still standing at a safe distance away. Three men walk slowly toward him, but they seem as afraid of him as he is of them. They are experienced rangers and know that he is young, but he still outweighs them by 8,000 pounds. As they get closer, Mosi senses their hesitation and lies on the ground. The men do not hear it, but Yama is calling to Mosi, reassuring him.

The men are wearing gloves, and one is holding tin snips. While two of them work to cut the wire, the other removes his gloves and touches Mosi's trunk. The ranger has studied elephant behavior for years but has never touched one. Mosi's trunk is like nothing he's ever felt, like layers of muscle sliding over a coiled spring. It feels so strong. Together the men remove the snare and run back toward the vehicles where they wait and watch. Mosi heaves himself up to stand and walks toward Yama. Mosi stops in front of Yama, who touches Mosi's head and back. He gently inspects the injury to Mosi's trunk. After several minutes, the two elephants turn and walk back in the direction from which they came. As the elephants disappear into a stand of trees, the people finally leave.

Mosi will always have a small hole in his trunk, but it wasn't severed. In time, the delicate tissue will heal around the wound, and he will learn to pull the muscles together to close the hole as he drinks.

His trunk is incomprehensibly strong because of its thick layers of muscle fibers, but its structural integrity is more complicated than that. The skin folds and wrinkles of the trunk serve a different purpose here than the water distributing crevices of the rest of Mosi's body. These are spaces that stretch and contract, interspersed with tough skin that isn't flexible, providing protection while allowing for movement. The trunk is also strong enough to toss a cape buffalo that weighs 1,500 pounds. The deep folds of Mosi's trunk help to distribute the load across an area, making the muscles less likely to collapse under weight. His trunk is an engineering marvel. The elephant is clearly an animal of great power. The combined strength and flexibility of the trunk makes it an animal of grace. The structural compromise will affect the lower third of Mosi's trunk. Though his trunk will never be as strong as it was, Mosi is lucky. He would not be the first elephant to die from a snare injury, nor would he be the last.

Over the next few months, Mosi recovers from the days without much food or water. He can use his trunk again to strip leaves or pull up plants. He stays even closer to Yama now, his patient protector. They have reunited with the bachelor group and are traveling again. Mosi swims and plays with the other young males whenever he can. While they roughhouse in the water, Mosi is careful to keep his trunk tucked under his chin, out of harm's way. Usually, Yama stands nearby and waits or eats. Today he has wandered to the edge of a stand of trees and is foraging there.

A cool breeze comes down from the escarpment to the west. Yama is quietly pulling leaves from the trees. He does not worry much about trucks here, especially during the day, so he does not pay attention until the truck is very close. Then he realizes it is too close. He turns to run but is hit by a dart and within minutes he falls.

The women and men in the truck get out and take an admiring survey over Yama. While they monitor his heart rate and temperature, they measure his tusks and look in his mouth at his block-like teeth. They put a needle into one of his big ear veins and take a sample of his blood and a stool sample from his rectum. Then they fit a radio collar onto his neck.

The humans ready themselves to leave and administer an injection that will reverse the tranquilizer. They drive to a safe distance and then wait for the big elephant to rouse. The veterinarian watches him closely with binoculars, counting the rise and fall of Yama's chest. When he goes too long without a breath, the humans hurry back to him, giving him another dose of reversal agent and monitoring desperately for a pulse. The veterinarian gets her emergency ventilator and delivers oxygen to Yama, but it is of no use, he never rouses. They realize that Yama is dead and gather around him, stunned and quiet, for several minutes.

The humans collect the collar. They must go back to the research station and get equipment to remove Yama's tusks so that they don't end up on the black market or laundered as legal trophies.

By this time, Mosi has gone looking for Yama and follows him by scent. He calls to Yama over and over again but gets no response. He finds Yama lying on the ground near a stand of trees. Mosi starts by inspecting Yama with his trunk, touching his face and mouth, then pushes on the big elephant with his feet. He walks around and then backs up to touch Yama with his foot pads, searching for signs of life. Mosi feels no breath, no heartbeat. He feels no rush of blood inside Yama's vessels. He understands that Yama is dead.

When the humans return to Yama, they find him covered in branches and leaves. Mosi and the other young males have done this. The humans uncover him and begin the process of removing his tusks. None of them have ever done this before, and they are not happy about it. They start on his left tusk with a chisel and mallet to remove the soft flesh of his face from around the alveolar socket that sets deep into his jaw. The chisel and mallet are slow going, so they switch to a machete, making a rhythmic thwacking sound as it cuts into his tissue. This part of his face is formed by lots of muscle at the base of his trunk. They remove enough to expose Yama's jaw and then try to chip through the bone that surrounds the alveolus. They pull repeatedly on the tusk, jerking Yama's head around, but can't get it out. They cut deep under the alveolus and higher into the jaw. Little bits of bone dust and blood fill the air, but still the tusk does not come out. They use Yama's head as a counterweight. Four of them stand around his head, take hold of part of the tusk, and pull directly up against gravity. Finally, the tusk releases from its socket and Yama's head falls back to the ground with a thud.

The right tusk is even more difficult because that side of his head lies against the ground, and they don't have a good way to move his head. They should have done that tusk first. Two of them hold Yama's head in position as the others take turns again removing the soft tissue and then the bone of his jaw around the socket. Finally, they remove the second tusk and load the pair into the back of the truck.

Mosi is nearby, hidden in the trees. He hears and smells it all. After the humans have gone, Mosi returns. He stands with the big elephant for several hours, touching his body, his tusks, and resting his trunk on Yama's head. Finally, he replaces the branches over Yama's body.

The bachelor group is quiet and subdued while they stay nearby for a couple of days. Eventually they continue their journey, moving closer toward the river as the dry season approaches. Hyenas feast on Yama's body. Vultures will be next.

DURING THE LATE 19TH AND EARLY 20TH CENTURIES, *several European countries invaded and colonized ninety percent of the African continent, much of which had been debilitated by the slave trade. Norman Carr was part of the colonial British diaspora of Central and Southern Africa. He was born in Mozambique in 1912 but as a young man lived in different locales within the region, including Nyasaland and Northern Rhodesia which are now Malawi and Zambia.*

Zambia is a land of Chiefdoms where people have tribal identities. The Chief is custodian of the land and cares for the needs of his people. In 1950, Carr was working as a ranger in the Luangwa Valley when he and Chief Nsefu of the Kunda people agreed to establish part of the Kunda tribal land as a public game-viewing reserve and conservation area. Later, additional land was set aside to establish South Luangwa National Park.

The idea of conservation-based tourism that benefits local people through jobs and community investment is credited to Carr. Income from tourism helped him to establish the Kapani School Project based in Mfuwe. The program was initially intended to provide books and uniforms for students. Now it sponsors more than eighty students from primary to college levels. There is also a girls' club and a home-based program for the education of children with physical and mental disabilities.

Part of Carr's vision was non-consumptive tourism as an alternative to hunting. He was noteworthy for not carrying a gun routinely during his work as a ranger or warden. Carr also started a Save the Rhino campaign in 1975, when rhinoceros were suffering from rampant illegal hunting. Despite those efforts, black rhinos were declared extinct from Zambia in 1998 but were reintroduced in the early 2000s. This population still lives in an isolated area inside North Luangwa National Park. The rhino population is growing, and none of the rhinos or the rangers who protect them have been killed since the reintroduction.

7. *Ecology*

SEPTEMBER

Stary and Mulenga's daughter, Chansa, signed up for a program at school to work with a group from Lusaka collecting local ecology data. Once a week during the dry season Chansa visits a mopane stand recording any birds or caterpillars on the trees, the high temperature, and any animals. The group provided her with a camera to take photos of the animals or any tracks, including those of human animals. Chansa uploads the photos to a site where people around the world can access them.

Chansa and the other volunteers have been taught to analyze the footprints for specific species, to determine who has been using the mopane thickets and under what conditions. The researchers will keep track of nutrients and pH of the soil, the monthly rainfall near each stand of interest, and other data. They hope to collect data for several years; it's difficult to see patterns in a year or two, especially when the conditions of one year impact life in the next.

As Chansa walks down the main road to and from school every day with her friends, all wearing their dark green uniforms and carrying backpacks, Stary can spot her from a distance by her special walk. She was born with the bones of her right ankle fused together. Stary recognizes her footprints when he sees them in the dirt, one flat on the ground and one a little sideways. Maybe every father's daughter stands out in a crowd, even if she does not walk with a hitch, but he feels a knot of pride in his chest when he sees her. Like an elephant, Chansa cannot jump with that right leg, but it doesn't seem to slow her down.

The coolest months have given up for the year. In a few weeks, when the heat perseverates and the water dries, Stary will rent the water truck again. When he can, he will take his children to the water hole to see the elephants. Now he looks forward to the dry season when he can be elephant caretaker.

If there is to be a future for elephants in this part of the world, his children's generation will have to know the elephants as his father did. They will have to learn their sounds, their warnings. They will need to predict elephant behavior. He is worried that this knowledge and the ways of coexistence will disappear. The culture around elephants now includes both fear and reverence, so there is still a chance. Stary does not want fear to win. He cannot make the sounds like his father could, but he can teach his children to listen, and learn that the sounds have meaning.

Stary and Chansa use an ancient elephant path to get to the mopane stand where she collects data. One day, they see Lua and her family a few hundred meters away to the side of the path in an open area of grass. The elephants are relaxing, leisurely making their way across the patch of savanna.

Stary recognizes Lua's tusk that curls up and sticks out to the side. He and Chansa stop and sit under a tree, quietly watching the elephant family. Stary tells her of the first time he met the elephants. She hears the intensity in his soft voice as he tells his story again, as he points out which elephants were stuck and what he did. But then he realizes the stately adolescent female is gone and the adolescent male isn't the same elephant he remembers. This one is smaller and seems more pensive. He feels that something heartbreaking has happened.

Sometimes Chansa sees elephants on the outskirts of the village. She likes seeing them, but they all look the same to her. She enjoys hearing how her father knows each one as an individual, and how they interact. They watch as Moyo and Rumphi play. Occasionally Sumina reaches out to Lua, touching her face.

Sumina caught Stary's scent before she saw him moving on the edge of her vision. Chansa's scent is unfamiliar, but she knows they are safe near Stary. The elephants do not acknowledge their presence, but they do not leave. Their two admirers keep a respectful distance.

The elephants wade into a small pool with water plants and eat their way across. The little ones follow their mothers as they move through the water. When they exit the other side, Moyo and Rumphi are completely dark with wet skin.

Getting late in the afternoon, Stary and Chansa need to be done before dusk when the night animals come out. They reluctantly leave the elephants and continue to the mopane stand. There are no caterpillars there now, but she checks the leaves and can see the eggs underneath. Eating the fully developed caterpillars before they metamorphosize into emperor moths can help animals survive the lean season at the end of the dry months. Even human animals rely on them for protein at that time of year, some say they taste like chicken, others like steak or even potato chips. Of course, it depends on how they're cooked. When the tree is full of caterpillars, Mulenga will come and harvest them for sale in the market.

The emperor moth favors the mopane tree to sustain its offspring as the eggs progress through the instar stages to adulthood. Like elephants, caterpillars have a long coevolutionary history with the tree. When the caterpillars completely defoliate a tree, it grows back with more small leaves, completely replacing what was eaten and adding new shoots for future growth.

Mopane can take the form of a tall, narrow tree, or shorter scrub brush. Once the mopane reaches tree height, it's largely resistant to a change in structure, but during its juvenile stage, defoliation can shape the tree into its shorter form. Caterpillars and elephants can cause these changes, especially if food is scarce and elephants overbrowse the trees. Though the shrubby form may not be as pleasing to the human eye as the taller tree, it provides reachable food for small animals who would otherwise struggle to get nutrients during the dry season—the interplay of living things.

Humans, who use mopane wood for heat or to make charcoal for cooking can also shape mopane into a shrub. In this form, it does not reproduce but is remarkably resilient. Because browsing pressure is part of the mopane's evolutionary history, the activity of caterpillars, human, or nonhuman animals rarely creates long-term damage that threatens the life of the tree. Though mopane only needs low rainfall to survive, under conditions of heavy use, presence of moisture in the soil largely determines whether the trees can recover. Soil nutrients are taken in with water, so rainfall is important both for the health of the plants and better nutrition in the leaves for animals who eat them.

Mopane seeds aren't usually spread by elephants other than when the tacky seedpods get stuck to their feet or they carry branches around. These seeds are also not primed by an elephant gut the way some seeds are. Being soaked by rain causes the seeds to germinate, but they need a second rainfall to grow. Sporadic and unreliable rainfall can kill the seedlings. If there is too much time in-between the first and second rain, they all die rather than simply lying dormant for longer before germinating.

Chansa takes her data logbook with her everywhere and makes notes in the back when she sees an animal or learns something new about a plant. She carries a spark, ignited by her mother's love of plants and her father's love of animals. Chansa has never built mental boundaries between herself and nature. She doesn't see a world of humans and a world of animals. She sees a world of living things, tiny and mighty, each with a role to play. She feels a part of it all.

Chansa is learning to see the subtleties of life around her, and someday, if the world she knows survives, she'll learn to listen to the birds for

signals about animals hidden in trees or long grass. She'll feel the wind to know from which direction to approach animals undetected. She'll smell the wild basil or the popcorn-scented urine mark of an elusive leopard. She'll know when the sly, spotted cat was there before her and moved on.

At school, Chansa learned the mopane trees release tannins to communicate with each other, sending the bitter chemicals into the air when animals begin to browse. Nearby trees receive the signals and increase their own tannin production before the animals have even taken a bite. Elephants move toward the trees from downwind, starting to browse while moving upwind to get to as many trees as they can before the tannins get too high and taste bad. But the trees have another line of defense—a web of fungi woven through the soil that responds to the plants' chemical defenses and communicates to the other mopane through their roots, like an old telephone line. It's an evolutionary dance, with attack and retreat, intrigue, and strategy.

Chansa knows that the plants react and respond, their chemical discourse generating protection for self and other trees. This warning system requires investment of individual resources to generate and release the chemical signals in response to being eaten—a sacrifice for collective survival.

After Chansa logs her data, she and Stary lie on their backs in the stand of trees, watching small, yellow butterflies flit above them. They enjoy the silence until the light begins to change. On their way home they see the metal roofs of the village shining in the evening sun, little flecks of welcoming light. As they pass the maize fields, reaped, and not yet cleared for planting, they're surrounded by a warm golden glow.

Human and nonhuman animals have coexisted here since humans first spread out from the Great Rift Valley just to the north. Animals were largely safe in Africa until foreigners brought guns to the continent and they could be killed from a distance.

In addition to helping popularize modern hunting in Africa, Theodore Roosevelt founded the National Park System of the United States, the first of its kind in the world. The parks were developed around the concept that protecting land means removing people living there. Native people who inhabited lands such as Yellowstone and Yosemite, among many other areas, were forcibly removed. When national parks were established in Africa, that same model was used. Local people were removed from the land, some of whom had lived in dynamic balance with wildlife and the ecosystem for countless generations.

Research into the effectiveness of traditional conservation strategies, from local to continental scale, shows that conservation works. This is true for habitat restoration, establishment of protected areas, and sustainable ecosystem management. But protecting an area doesn't require removing people who are stewards of the land simply by their traditional ways of living. In some cases, supporting those people in enforcing their land rights, or legal restrictions on natural resource exploitation by outsiders can be powerful conservation tools. Local populations can also be adept at sharing space with wildlife, or at least living in successful avoidance of each other. This type of knowledge is important for developing strategies of coexistence.

If Lua and other elephants can't survive the heat and its changes, the savanna won't support life as it has since elephants first shaped it millions of years ago. For example, Lua's digestion of only about half of the plant material she eats means that the biomass gets recycled back into the ecosystem, helping plants regenerate, especially in areas with poor soil. In some places, her dung provides a critical return of nitrogen, phosphorus, carbon, and potassium to the earth—nutrients which can be the primary limiting factor of vegetation growth. When Stary and Chansa see patches of green on the savanna floor left behind after Lua's dung has decomposed, they know it's a sign of a much larger process at work.

Without the ecosystem services of Lua and the family, woody shrubs will outcompete the grasses, leaving many herbivores without enough to eat. Predators of the savanna will quickly suffer next. Wildlife like lions and leopards are not the only ones—local people in some rural areas hunt antelope as an important source of food. Antelope are more abundant where there are elephants.

Large trees in the patchwork of forests across the savanna store high amounts of carbon, a safeguard against climate change. With their selective browsing of smaller competition, Lua and family aid growth of these trees. Their loss will take longer to feel. That effect of elephant absence may only be noticed after existing trees die and don't replace themselves. Birds and primates will lose their homes in the canopy. Amphibians and reptiles of the forest floor will lose their breeding ground and refuge. The land may still have life, but likely only small animals that can survive on woody shrubs in dry climates will endure.

When the trees are gone, women will no longer be able to collect the marula fruit for sale in the market. Mulenga also relies on myrrh to protect her family from intestinal worms and the fever tree for malaria. Disease-carrying mosquitoes are already expanding their altitude range in sub-Saharan Africa as the heat extends up the slopes of the mountains. Fewer birds also mean more mosquitoes, another spiral. The plants of the savanna, and all over the world, provide gifts of food, medicine, and protection from weather; all they ask for is sun, soil, and rain.

UNDER BRITISH COLONIAL RULE, *schools run by Rhodesians were illegal, but education was not, unlike in other colonized African states. The Democratic Republic of the Congo (DRC), just to the north of Zambia, was a slave state as governed by famously brutal King Leopold of Belgium. At first, the colonized Congo was essentially the personal property of Leopold and existed as a state of terror. He demanded that local people harvest and deliver vast quantities of ivory and rubber. If an individual failed to supply enough, his hand was cut off by local enforcers, or he might simply be killed. Several million, perhaps as many as ten million,*

Congolese people were murdered during the reign of Leopold, with millions more fleeing to neighboring countries.

After Belgium officially declared the Congo a colony, conditions were not much better. As of independence in 1960, the DRC had fewer than twenty university graduates in a population of 13 million. There were highly educated Congolese both at home and abroad, but the reality of sudden rule by the undereducated and inexperienced was common during the period of anti-colonial revolution which spread across the African continent in the 1950s and 60s.

Zambia is surrounded by countries that did not undergo peaceful transitions of power. Each of these countries has a unique story of independence and a legacy of violence that continue to shadow life there. Part of this legacy involves the international tendency to accept, or support, the violent establishment of government, rather than establishment by more democratic processes.

Northern Rhodesia's transition to the country we now know as Zambia was much more peaceful than most of its neighbors. Years of nonviolent uprising led to the colonial ruling party's inclusion of native-African-led United National Independence Party (UNIP) in the country's elections. This does not mean that people in Northern Rhodesia did not die on both sides of the struggle for independence, just that violence was not the strategy of the revolutionary effort there. The relatively peaceful transition of power to UNIP was, in part, due to external forces, but the party's success ultimately led to universal suffrage and establishment of Zambia as a republic.

Societal upheavals that accompany armed conflicts are devastating for both people and animals. Wildlife may be victims of guns or land mines, and ivory sale has been known to fund militias, like blood diamonds. But wildlife is usually a more indirect casualty of human conflict, with resource destruction and loss of land and habitat. Elephants who flee conflict for safety can end up living like refugees, waiting for an opportunity to go home which may or may not come. Areas of relative safety become havens for wildlife, which, at a critical mass, can then lead to new conflicts between humans and displaced animals. Any instability within the region can negatively affect all life there. Everything is connected.

8. A *Life Apart*

When Tunya and the other six young females arrive in the United States, they spend another few weeks together in the care of veterinarians before they are sent to their respective zoo facilities, some as pairs and others alone. Tunya is moved to a zoo in the Midwest, where she is the first of their planned African elephant herd. The zoo has had Asian elephants for many years, and the staff is excited to work with an African elephant for the first time.

Tunya is placed in a large enclosure with metal bars inside the elephant house. To her right is the exterior wall of the building. To her left is an enclosure shared by two adult female elephants. Tunya recognizes their comforting rumbles, but they also make sweet chirping sounds that are new to her. Tunya could touch the two of them if she wanted to, but for now she stays on her own next to the wall.

Her caretakers know Tunya will need a lot of training to function well at the zoo, and they try to reward her with sweet treats. They want her to come forward to the front of her enclosure and raise her feet one at a time so they can be inspected for injury or infection every day. Tunya does not respond. Her food is in a trough which can be accessed from the front by her caretakers. She waits until no one is around before she will eat, although she doesn't eat much. She's lost her muscular build over these last few months, enough to cause worry.

One day, as a caretaker fills Tunya's trough, he doesn't notice that she's closer than usual. With a quick flick of her trunk, Tunya undercuts the left side of his jaw. The strike sends him flying backward. His head bangs on the floor and the bucket of food skitters across the floor with a racket. Other than the elephants, no one's around to notice.

He gets up slowly and surveys himself, deciding that he isn't seriously injured. He has worked with elephants for years and knows they can be unpredictable. He makes a mental note to be more careful and doesn't fill out an incident report. And he hopes he can win Tunya over with kindness and sweets.

The elephant exhibit has a big yard with trees and a wading pool that the other elephants enjoy. The young ones often put on a show for the crowd, who can watch from a lookout above. It's a favorite spot for zoo visitors. The zoo staff try to give Tunya some time in the elephant yard, to walk around and explore, but she rarely goes. When they clear the yard and open the door to let her out, she stands in the corner of her enclosure and sways side to side.

Tunya's neighbors, Molly and Annie, have both been zoo elephants since they were small. Molly was born in Thailand and caught in the wild. As elephant mothers do, Molly's mother put up a fight for her baby and was killed. Molly can remember the smell of her mother and of the land, but she accepted captivity and has always been pretty easy to handle. Annie was born in a zoo with great fanfare and excitement from the zoo staff and the community. When her mother rejected her shortly after her birth, Annie was raised by humans who bottle-fed her and kept her company in shifts until she was a year old. They tried to show her love as her mother should have.

Annie has grown into a fine-looking elephant, but she has always been a little bit neurotic. She also has a chronic injury that causes her to drag her right back leg. Molly's presence helps to keep her calm. Annie and Molly have been a bonded pair for more than five years. The two can feel Tunya's despair that pervades the elephant house. It's not normal for an elephant to sway repetitively in silence, and if Tunya could hide, she would. The constant vibration of the zoo, shrill of human voices, and flurry of activity is too much.

Tunya's feet become the focus of her existence. She feels every person's footfall, every shout. She does not habituate to it because she is trying to feel for something familiar, for her mother. The only thing that makes sense to her is rain. It feels different through the hard concrete than through soil, but it's still rain. She knows it through her feet.

Elephant feet are not made for standing on hard ground. Tunya develops a sore on her left back foot and begins to limp. She hasn't responded well to her training and isn't getting regular foot checks. Zoo staff have been trying to figure out how to get her the routine veterinary care that she needs but have been hesitant to sedate her. Tunya moves so little during the day that they don't realize she has a foot sore until one morning when they find her lying down.

Humans and other mammals actively exhale and passively inhale. Air fills the empty lungs without the use of muscles because of pressure differences within the chest cavity, inside and outside of the lungs. Tunya's lungs are attached to her chest wall, another peculiarity of elephant anatomy. She must actively exhale and actively inhale. This requires effort and makes it hard to breathe while lying down, which, in turn, makes it difficult for her to stand up from the ground. Any injury that causes an elephant to lie down can be fatal.

Caretakers are finally forced to sedate her to treat her infected foot before the infection gets into her blood. They give her an injection of antibiotics, and she will need regular monitoring. Tunya likes bananas and will be offered more than her share for the next few days, attempts to entice her to move closer so they can look at her feet. Despite her cravings, she doesn't pick up the bananas. They have to sedate her two more times. Tunya's foot recovers, but this has not increased her trust. Zoo staff agree to start Tunya on a daily antidepressant in the hope that it will help her respond better to training.

Molly has started calling to Tunya and trying to comfort her. The caretakers cannot hear it, but they feel the waves of Molly's voice in their chests as the two elephants stand facing each other on either side of the bars. Over time, Tunya gets used to the constant hum, the new rhythm of the world around her. The caretakers start finding her on the side of her enclosure close to Molly and Annie. Gradually, Tunya eats more, and she goes from not eating and underweight, to overweight.

One evening, after the crowd is gone for the day, the caretakers move Molly and Annie into the elephant yard and then nervously open Tunya's door. Tunya steps out of the enclosure and as she enters the yard, runs toward Molly while trumpeting out hesitant squeaky exclamations. Molly greets her with touches and rumbles. Their language may be different, but some things about elephants are universal.

The caretakers are overjoyed; perhaps Tunya will start settling into life here. They start allowing the three elephants time together in the yard on a regular basis. Tunya even gets into the water to play with Annie. Though Annie is full-grown, Tunya is bigger. When Tunya reaches her full adult size, she will outweigh Annie by about two thousand pounds.

YEARS AGO, THE ZOO ATTEMPTED TO BREED ANNIE with the resident male. In his powerfully aggressive height of musth, the big bull knocked her down and injured her. Unlike females in the wild, inside the enclosure Annie was unable to get away from him, and she has had a leg injury ever since.

Historically there have been very few male elephants in US zoos. Almost all elephants have been imported from the wild (and almost all from Asia, although it's now prohibited). Males were considered too difficult to handle in captivity, incomprehensibly big and strong. The few males in zoos were mostly born there, though this was rare. There are many reasons for breeding difficulty, including that there are not many males to breed and because males and females are not often in the same space at the same time. By the age of four or five, males were typically kept in solitary conditions to keep those around them safe.

In the interest of allowing them to socialize, some young males are given hormonal vaccines to permanently prevent full adult development and aggression. Reducing their feed to keep them malnourished or minimizing access to water so that they stay mildly dehydrated can also stop their normal hormonal surges. Even when bulls are allowed to enter musth and given the opportunity to mate, the elephants may choose not to. Zookeepers call it behavioral incompatibility. For all these reasons, it's taken enormous effort to maintain the elephant population in US zoos with artificial insemination and in vitro fertilization.

Over the next few months, zoo staff decide to move forward with breeding Tunya. That was the intention from the beginning—for her to start a new African elephant herd at the zoo. Specialists give Tunya hormones to induce estrus, and then she undergoes artificial insemination. They have tried this twice with Molly, but she has never successfully conceived.

It's not easy to tell if an elephant is pregnant. At one point, they sedate Tunya to give her a thorough physical exam and take a blood sample. They are elated when her pregnancy test is positive. African elephant zoo births are almost unheard of. This will be the biggest event, and the biggest baby the zoo has ever seen.

Tunya's mood becomes entirely dependent on Molly and Annie. Their caretakers stay away from Tunya as much as they can because she becomes visibly agitated in their presence. They don't allow her around elephants other than her pair of friends and she only goes into the yard when the zoo is closed to visitors. Her life develops a simple routine as the days pass.

The caretakers hope that having a baby to care for will help Tunya to accept life here, will soften her. They want her to be happy. Zoo staff cannot help thinking ahead to the long-term future of African elephants in the US. If the baby is a boy, someday his sperm can be used to build a genetic bank for African elephants and help perpetuate his species in zoos. He could exponentially increase the existing captive breeding potential. Of course, a girl may someday have babies of her own. Either way, there is not much that the public likes more than a new elephant baby.

By the end of her 22-month gestation, Tunya's body has widened. Her caretakers move her to a large enclosure in a separate, unused building where they have easier access to her if there are any problems during the birth. When she goes into labor, she can't get comfortable or hold still. She paces, then tries to lie down, but can't and she struggles to get up. Stress secretions flow from the sides of her head; she is confused and visibly distressed. Staff watch her from a safe distance. When the baby finally arrives and drops to the floor, Tunya turns and attacks him, stomping on him with her front feet. Sometimes this happens in captive elephants, and her caretakers are ready. They shoot her with a tranquilizer dart, only because it is an emergency. After Tunya slumps down, her caretakers go into the enclosure and get the tiny elephant. They do their best to resuscitate him but are unsuccessful.

Tunya's caretakers grieve for the short and brutal life of her baby, a prized animal, defenseless against attack. Loved, but not shown love.

Tunya becomes overtly aggressive any time people are around. She bangs on her food trough and starts hurting herself. Even Molly can't calm her.

Zoo staff give up their idea of starting an African elephant herd. They find a smaller zoo that has been looking for an elephant for years. Their resident Asian elephant died young, and Tunya will replace her. As the only elephant, they can devote singular attention to her well-being. They are also going to design a new exhibit around her. The lion, zebra, and giraffe yards will be moved closer together. A display will teach visitors about the savanna and the importance of conservation there. They will collect and donate money for conservation efforts in Africa.

The move is uneventful, but Tunya is more withdrawn than ever. She sways side to side incessantly. Her new caretakers can tell that she is developing sores on her feet, and they must sedate her for treatment. Before long, she begins to bang her head on the wall and bars of her enclosure. The zoo veterinarians add a low dose of barbiturate to her antidepressant every day to keep her calm. After some time, they add another sedative. She still sways some, but she no longer injures herself. She simply retreats to the back corner of her enclosure and mostly looks at the wall. Sometimes a bird gets stuck inside the elephant house and flies around her, but Tunya does not seem to notice.

A few months pass, and nothing changes much for Tunya. The zoo director paused the exhibit that was planned, something she had dreamed about for a long time. She meets with Tunya's caretakers, and they decide to contact a sanctuary for elephants who have retired from zoos or the entertainment industry. Representatives from the sanctuary come to visit. Tunya would be the youngest elephant under their care. At the sanctuary, with several acres to roam outside on grass and in the trees, she could live another forty years or more. Unlike their other elephants, Tunya has never learned the skills of an elephant in captivity, regular foot checks and other routine veterinary care. It will be a challenge, but they cannot bear for Tunya to continue living the life that has been created for her or for her to be put down.

There is an older African elephant, Sadie, who also lives at the sanctuary. She was imported from Africa when she was barely weaned from her mother and was meant to be in the movies. Sadie never turned into the star that her owner was hoping for, as she was so much bigger and more expensive to feed than her smaller, distant cousins. Also, interest in animal welfare led to increased regulations and protections for animal actors.

During the day Sadie wanders the hills and woods of the sanctuary, often wallowing in the pond in the afternoon. She can do what she wants and eat what she chooses. When Tunya arrives, they will each have an enclosure in the barn where they will spend every night. For now, Tunya will be kept in the barnyard during the day. Hopefully she will acclimate to the place and to Sadie; maybe someday they can share the acres to roam.

The zoo staff who relinquish Tunya decide not to replace her. They hire a consultant to help them build an immersive virtual exhibit to showcase African wildlife. Visitors walk through the display, feeling what it is like to stand before these grand animals, to see an elephant care for her baby or to feel the roar of a lion close enough to make their hair stand on end. Zoo guests can follow painted dogs on a hunt. They will get to experience the savanna at night, to hear the whoop of the hyena and watch a honey badger catch a snake or a bushbaby hunt a scorpion. The energy of the savanna will shimmer with the mysterious animals, small and elusive, who live there. Visitors will see how the warming earth has changed and will continue to change the landscape and how animals can or cannot cope. They will see how the populations of animals diminish as their habitats die and they have no water.

In the sanctuary, Tunya is introduced to a new set of people, smells, and sounds. Her new caretakers watch nervously while Tunya stands quietly in the yard. She's still receiving her daily prescriptions, from which they hope to wean her over the next few months. What will she need that they haven't foreseen?

Tunya's new humans are about to return to the sanctuary office when they see Tunya raise her head. She snaps her ears out and with bobs of her trunk is actively pulling in scent. In a few minutes they see a gray figure walk out of the trees from the back acres. Sadie felt the big truck come and go and comes to investigate. As she walks directly to the fence, Tunya moves toward her. The two elephants stop and face each other and stand like that while the sun goes down, sensing and communicating things only they can know. It is the first time Tunya has been outside for a sunset in more than four years.

As it gets dark, Sadie walks into the barn and into her enclosure. Tunya follows Sadie on the other side of the fence, into her new space in the barn. The caretakers close each door and head home for the night. When they return the next morning, they feel shudders in the air. Sadie and Tunya are having a call and response discussion. They release each elephant from her enclosure. A fence still separates the two, with Tunya in the small barnyard and Sadie in the bigger yard that reaches into the back acres. The elephants stand sideways next to each other on either side of the heavy bars. Sadie reaches her trunk over to Tunya. They explore each other's faces. Sadie feels Tunya's broken tusk.

Sadie walks to the gate. She grasps the chain with her trunk, rattles it, and looks at her caretakers. The sanctuary staff pride themselves on allowing the elephants as much autonomy as possible. Sadie is clearly communicating her demand, but the staff are nervous there might be a conflict. Will one of the elephants get injured? Tunya hasn't moved, standing with her trunk draped over the fence. Two members of staff climb over the fence into the bigger yard that opens into the back acres. They tell Sadie to move back, and she gives them a safe distance. They open the gate and then quickly hop back over the fence. As Tunya walks through the gate Sadie turns to the back acres. The two elephants move placidly into the trees and out of sight.

ELEPHANTS CLEARLY FEEL JOY AND GRIEF. *They get frustrated and have tantrums. They have friends. Elephants have individual personalities, but as a group are known for their peaceful nature and their capacity to have loving relationships with each other as well as animals of other species. Author Eric Scigliano claims, "Most of all, they resemble (perhaps even surpass) us on the depth of their familial attachments and affective communications." Can an animal really feel more deeply than we do?*

Conservationist and author Lawrence Anthony appreciated the emotional character of elephants and their responsiveness to emotion in others. For several days Anthony and his crew had been capturing and containing nyala, small deer-like animals, in a holding pen. The men were going to move the nyala to a private reserve. On the night before the move, the matriarch of a local elephant family opened the gate and stood aside to let the nyala out. Anthony believed she was responding to their distress call.

Wild elephants may also help injured humans, guarding them, or even moving them to safety. Dame Daphne Sheldrick was once badly injured by a wild elephant whom she had mistaken for an elephant she had raised as an orphan. After approaching and touching the other elephant, Sheldrick was thrown onto some rocks and broke her leg. The elephant then seemed to realize Sheldrick wasn't a threat and was injured; she tried to lift Sheldrick back onto her feet.

Scientists can study bonding behaviors, stress hormones, communication, the movement of elephants across a continent, and the intricate ecology of life inside an ecosystem; but they can't explain why a full-grown bull elephant, in all his glory, would shift his feet out of the way so that a tortoise could stay on its path without adjusting its course.

Author Edward Wilson claimed that our sense of wonder grows exponentially: the greater the knowledge, the deeper the mystery. As science has changed from characterizing animals as simplistic organisms without thought or emotion to acknowledging them as sentient beings with consciousness and volition, they have indeed grown in mystery. We can appreciate animals' emotional lives. We're allowed to marvel at the individual character of elephants and at their remarkable, mysterious existence—a knowing wonder.

One of the mysteries of elephant life is their seeming understanding of death. Elephants may urgently try to lift or rouse injured conspecifics. Ian Douglas-Hamilton relayed a gruesome story of an elephant mother who was dying from a culler's bullet; she placed the tip of her trunk into the hand of the man who was about to slit the throat of her calf. They also demonstrate clear expression of grief for companions, elephant or otherwise.

For philosopher Vinciane Despret, the question is not whether animal grief is the same as human grief, the appropriate question about animal grief is, "What does this ask of us?" We know an enormous amount about what animals need to live good lives. What does that knowledge ask of us?

9. *Fire*

NOVEMBER

Lua's life stages are very familiar—childhood, adolescence, adulthood. Her memory includes changes that have unfolded over decades. Decades when the rains were better. Decades before humans moved into permanent settlements along the edge of the valley. Decades when hearing guns was common and others when it was not. Decades with her mother and then after her mother was gone. A decade with Tunya before she vanished. If Lua and Tunya were reunited again, after decades apart, they would know each other only by scent.

How other species perceive time is a mystery. Lua lives on the elephant timescale, slow movements and the passing of days determined by the rhythm of life around her. How does she experience the lapse of minutes, days, or decades? Is her perception of time affected by the fact that she never forgets? Is yesterday just as important as ten years ago?

In the weeks after Tunya's disappearance, Lua grew to understand that Tunya would not return. Her grief for Tunya seems to have no timescale; it has an infinite life of its own.

She and Moyo separated from their small family and stayed among the trees for several days. Lua's grief was thick around her; Moyo was distressed and confused. Finally, when Lua had little milk left and Moyo's hunger would not abate, they found Sumina again. She and

Rumphi were together with the male orphan, no longer relegated to the periphery. The two males, one baby and one adolescent, had little energy to play but had nonetheless bonded. Sumina seemed to accept the new male as her own.

Sumina is becoming a more confident leader, although she will never be a strong matriarch as Lua was. The range of their home is smaller now, partly because of Sumina, but mostly because of things out of her control.

All animals in the area are hungry and skittish. They scatter in response to sounds or movement that would not have bothered them in the past. To the west, men still enter the park at night, hunting for meat. To the east, villages have become a dangerous refuge for animals without other options. Stary hasn't seen elephants around during the day, but he has heard about elephant night raids.

Other villagers are more worried about lions that have been coming into the village and taking livestock. A teenager from a nearby village went out on a recent evening, looking for missing cattle. A lioness leaped toward him from behind some bushes and he barely escaped up a tree. He stayed in the tree all night long until his father came to look for him. It's unusual for a lioness to attack a human, either adult or child, or even for her to come so close to a village. She may be driven by hunger or some unknown provocation. Now, everyone is too afraid to go outside except in the middle of the day.

Losing livestock is devastating, and most families here lack the resources to protect their animals at night. There have been retaliatory killings of two of the local pride males, which sends the local lion population into more chaos. An exception among felines, *Panthera leo* is the only social cat. Lionesses work together to hunt and to feed each other's offspring. But the social culture of lions puts them at risk in other ways. Each male in succession will try to kill the infants of a pride male who has been displaced. Male lions will not spare the genetic line of another male to protect the survival of the species. The retaliatory killings have left behind mostly scruffy adolescents who are not ready to hunt for themselves or for a pride.

Because there are too many dangerous animals close to the village, Chansa's parents won't allow her to continue her data collection in the mopane. She is sad that she can't continue and upset that the researchers won't understand why she didn't follow through with her work.

Sumina and Lua are also wary of the pressured and agitated lions. Well-fed lions wouldn't confront them, but desperate lions will, especially when the little elephants are struggling to keep up. This time of year is always the riskiest, but the current conditions make it easier to separate babies from their families, especially when their mothers are weak and not able to protect them.

The family stays within a small area along the eastern edge of the park boundary, close to the river like much of the wildlife. Food sources are dwindling, and Sumina will have to make a choice to stay and risk starvation or leave and risk dehydration and people.

The little food that the elephants find to eat is dry and not nutritious. The brittle scraps of plants aren't adequate as a source for mother's milk or as a supplement the little ones can eat. The elephants seem as if they are stuck in slow motion, trying not to waste energy on extra movements or creating heat.

Lua's stress is still so high that her cortisol hormone reduces her baseline production and nutritional content of her milk, especially a lower percentage of fat. She passes cortisol through her milk, adding to Moyo's high level, making her anxious and hungry. She agitatedly pushes on Lua's front legs with her head or kicks at Lua with her back feet. She tries to suckle from Sumina but is gently pushed away. If Sumina tries to feed both Rumphi and Moyo, both calves will die.

Elephant calves are supposed to be round and soft little bundles of energy. Moyo's eyes are sunken and dull, her skin sags. She has trouble getting up after resting, which she does most of the time. Sumina needs to lead her two young bulls to a different area but won't leave Lua and

Moyo behind. One day, Moyo lies down and can't get up again. Lua stands over her, making shade for Moyo as her little body finally gives up.

Lua's grief is already a deep pool out of which she cannot climb. They stay with Moyo's body for a couple of days, touching it, then covering it, and then simply standing in vigil. Then the small family moves on—the reluctant leader, her son, an adopted orphan, and Lua, who has lost all of her children despite being a strong and capable leader.

Stary knows about the hunters on the western edge of the park. He knows that the elephants are trapped. Perhaps his elephants will not return to the water hole this season as the heat rises and the water lowers. Perhaps he will lose his connection with the family. Perhaps he will not be able to introduce them to his other children.

Stary worries that without the skills of coexistence the animals and land will be lost.

Chansa has started a business in the village. From their chile plants she makes a paste and trades it to their neighbors. Stary teaches them to make chile-elephant dung briquettes to keep the elephants away.

One farmer in a nearby village got lights that flash when an animal walks too close. Stary has heard that the lights can change color, so they look different every night. Maybe it will work or maybe the elephants will get used to the lights and stop being afraid. He believes that elephants will never like chile.

Mulenga meets regularly with an agricultural advisor from the university in Mpika. For the last few years, Mulenga and Stary have portioned some of their fields for cassava in addition to maize. She knows about the effect of monoculture on diet and degradation to the soil. Crop diversity is good for nutrients in the body and the earth. Like many of their generation around the world, Stary and Mulenga's recent ancestors grew a greater variety of crops for local consumption. When the crops became a commodity for city markets, more resources were invested in fewer types of produce. Now they have trouble getting seeds for crops that used to be common there. Mulenga would like to add peanuts, which elephants do not eat, but other farmers have been losing their peanuts to fungus, one that becomes worse with higher temperatures. Mulenga will add soybeans instead. At her last meeting she also received sweet potato slips with the agreement to propagate them and give them away.

More than elephants, either unpredictable rains or heat can threaten widescale crop destruction. Local tradition of planting in October and November in anticipation of the coming rains has historically resulted in maximized maize yields, but now it leads to increased evaporation of water from the soil. Stary decides to plant the maize in stages. Later planting will save some evaporative loss in the fields and reduce the chance of losing an entire harvest from either heat or lack of rain. It also decreases the likelihood that elephants will disrupt a whole season's worth of crop at one time. He will also try pigeon peas which can be planted among the other crops to shade the soil from the relentless sun and reduce water demand.

Mulenga, now a leader in the village, helps her neighbors make decisions about crops and planting. Mulenga will do everything that she can to defend her family and her home, but she can't control the actions of people in faraway places.

Sumina and the family are moving north in the eastern section of the park under a cloudless expanse of blue sky; the air is so dry it feels brittle. The elephants sense a vibration through their feet. Sumina stops. First, she places her trunk on the ground and then lifts it into the air. The scent of fire is coming from the direction of the cultivated fields to the northwest, moving toward them with the wind. The family cannot see it yet, but a haze darkens the sky as the blaze rushes over the tinder of dry grass in its path.

Sumina signals the family to run southeast. They make it to the river, but the bank is too high for them to get down. Sumina also isn't certain that the water is low enough for Rumphi to cross and the area is a favorite of crocodiles. Sumina moves along the bank, searching in vain for a place where they can cross. She stops to think, feeling the fire within her body, the scent, the vibration, the roar of the flames, turning everything to ash. Now she can see the darkness of the sky, rising above the flashes of flame.

Sumina's only thought is to make it to the water, but she cannot figure out how to keep Rumphi safe. The rest of the family wait for a signal.

Lua turns away from them, facing the direction of the fire and lets out a great bellow. She moves north in parallel with the river as the family follows, the heat pricking their skin. Then Lua turns away from the water and runs several hundred meters to a low spot; a mopane thicket has been overbrowsed and is little more than stubs in the sandy soil.

The family stands clustered together in the middle of the dead thicket. Within minutes, the fire surges past, a wall of flame, but there is no fuel to burn around them. The inferno passes by as a shimmer of light and movement; the intensity in the air is all-encompassing, a blazing fury that reaches the river and burns out.

Flecks of ash float in the air, like sooty snowflakes falling around the elephants. It will take several days for the air and their lungs to clear.

The dark, thick smoke is visible to Stary and Mulenga. They stand outside with their children, grateful that their village was not in the path of the blaze. Behind the haze, the sun has a dull and eerie glow, but the dark sky does not cool the air.

After the fire is spent, Lua leads the family south along the river. Her usual senses are blunted, so she navigates by feel of the earth. She must find a new home for the next few weeks, away from the haze and the burned fodder. Not the best time of year to travel, and they still hear gunshots in the distance sometimes at night, but Lua weighs the best of the poor options.

The family walks together, a memory of elephants, across the dry earth. Grand, gray animals gently plodding across a brown landscape as the sun sets, silhouetting them with golden light. A few impalas are following at a distance. During the coming weeks they will all be trying one more time to hold on to life until the rains come, each year trying to survive longer without water than the last. This is life for the family as they negotiate the normality of loss and perpetual change. As the sun falls in the west, the air finally cools. The energy of the night is all around them as they step their soft feet silently onto the earth.

Acknowledgments

When I first sent Gregory Graalfs a manuscript about elephants and ecology, it was a tome of careful research and documentation. Surprisingly, he read the whole thing. Then he told me if I rewrote it as a narrative, he might be interested. Only when he followed up a few weeks later, and after I read *Ice Walker* multiple times, did I really consider giving it a try. This book only exists because of his idea and support throughout the process. For all of that, I am forever grateful. Thank you also to Bruce Rutledge for believing in the book and making it happen.

Thank you to Zoe Quinton for listening, enthusiasm, and guidance in making *Knowing Wonder* a stronger story. Todd Shimoda, thank you for your attention to detail, improving the structure of the book, and generally being a pleasure to work with. Thank you to an anonymous reviewer for your thoroughness and suggestions. Thanks to Catherine Doyle of PAWS, Matt Hartley of Zoo Solutions, and Emily McWilliam of BEES, for your time and expertise. Thank you to Alex George for your advice and unparalleled generosity of spirit. Communicating with people like James Raffan and Patrick Curry, both models of graciousness, was an unexpected pleasure in this process. Sincere thanks to all of you.

Thank you to Mark Friend, a friend indeed, for answering so many questions. Sherri Pelzel and Jane Fisher each spent an enormous amount of time reading and making suggestions. Their enthusiasm kept me going. I can still hear Sherri say, "I was never bored," even by my original tome of research.

My father, Warren Sapp, believed in this project long before it was a fully formed idea. Ryan Roe, thank you for your companionship, constant support, and participating in this journey. You are the kindest and most patient person I know. My mother, Betty Sapp, a very smart woman, read every draft of every version of the manuscript. She tirelessly responds to out-of-the-blue questions about word choice or phrasing and knows the proper use of the word *endemic*. Thank you. The book would also not exist without you.

Citations

AUTHOR'S NOTE

Knowing Wonder: An Elephant Story is a work of fiction that includes actual events and was inspired by real elephants and people. The story would not be possible without the work listed here. I am grateful to these authors and the people and animals who participated in their research.

PREFACE

1. Raffan, J. (2020). *Ice Walker*. Simon & Schuster.
2. Kingsnorth, P. (2017). *Confessions of a Recovering Environmentalist and Other Essays*. Graywolf Press, 80.

CHAPTER 1: IN THE VALLEY

1. **Finding water by smell:** Wood, M. (2022). African elephants can detect water from natural and artificial sources via olfactory cues. *Animal Cognition, 25*(1), 53-61.
2. **Possibility of water echolocation:** O'Connell-Rodwell, C.E., Wood, J.D., Rodwell, T.C., Puria, S., Partan, S.R., Keefe, R., Shriver, D., Arnason, B.T., & Hart, L.A. (2006). Wild elephant (Loxodonta africana) breeding herds respond to artificially transmitted seismic stimuli. *Behav Ecol Sociobiol*, 59, 842-850; Scigliano, E. (2002). *Love, War, and Circuses: That Age-Old Relationship between Elephants and Humans*. Bloomsbury, London, 31.
3. **Elephant digs and baboons maintain the wells:** Payne, K. (1998). *Silent Thunder: In the Presence of Elephants*. Penguin Books, New York, 253.
4. **Elephant play:** Moss, C. (1988). *Elephant Memories: Thirteen Years in the Life of an Elephant Family*. Ivy Books, New York; O'Connell-Rodwell, C.E. (2021). Why animals play. *Scientific American*, 325, 2; Poole, J.H., Granli, P.K. (2004). The visual, tactile, and acoustic signals of play in African savanna elephants. In *Endangered Elephants, past, present & future*. Jayewardene, Jayantha. (Ed.) Proceedings of the Symposium on Human Elephant Relationships and Conflicts, Sri Lanka, September 2003. Biodiversity & Elephant Conservation Trust, Colombo, 44-50.

5. **Foraging effects:** Pringle, R.M. (2008). Elephants as agents of habitat creation for small vertebrates at the patch scale. *Ecology*, 89 (1), 26-33.
6. **Birds live where elephants are:** Francis, R.J., Brandis, K.J., Kingsford, R.T., & Callaghan, C.T. (2020). Quantifying bird diversity at three sites of differing herbivore presence. *Journal of Ornithology;* Tripathy, H.G., Mzumara, T.I., Martin, R.O., Parr, C.L., Phiri, C., & Ryan, C.M. (2019). Dissimilar effects of human and elephant disturbance on woodland structure and functional bird diversity in the mopane woodlands of Zambia. *Landscape Ecol*, 34, 357-371.
6. **Elephants known by voice:** McComb, A., Moss, C., Sayialel, S., Baker, L. (2000). Unusually extensive networks of vocal recognition in African elephants. *Animal Behavior*, 59, 1103-1109.
7. **Elephant names:** Pardo, M.A., Fristrup, K., Lolchuragi, D.S. Poole, J.H., Granli, P., Moss, C., Douglas-Hamilton, I., & Wittemyer, G. (2024). African elephants address one another with individually specific name-like calls. *Nat Ecol Evol*, 8, 1353–1364; above research presented by: Pardo, M.A. (2023, June 13). Do elephants have names? Vocal labeling of individual conspecifics in African elephants. [Video]. Retrieved from Youtube.com https://youtube.com/watch?v=D2iKmmGAwCY. Simons Institute workshop: Decoding Communication in Nonhuman Species II.
8. **Family dynamics:** Lee, P.C., & Moss, C.J. (2011). Calf development and maternal rearing strategies. In Moss, C.J., Croze, H., & Lee, P.C. (Eds.) *The Amboseli Elephants: A Long-Term Perspective on a Long-Lived Mammal.* University of Chicago Press, 224-237.
9. Gravett, N., Bhagwandin, A., Sutcliffe, R., Landen, K., Chase, M.J., Lyamin, O.I., Siegel, J.M., & Manger, P.R. (2017). Inactivity/sleep in two wild free-roaming African elephant matriarchs—Does large body size make elephants the shortest mammalian sleepers? *Plos One*, 12(3).
10. Kinahan, A.A., Inge-Moller, R., Bateman, P.W. Kotze, A., & Scantlebury, M. (2007). Body temperature daily rhythm adaptations in African savanna elephants (Loxodonta africana). *Phyiol. Behav.*, 92 (4), 560-565.
11. **Elephant communication:** O'Connell-Rodwell, C.E., Wood, J.D., Wyman, M., Redfield, S. Puria, S. & Hart, L.A. (2012). Antiphonal vocal bouts associated with departures in free-ranging African elephant family groups (Loxodonta africana). *Bioacoustics*, 21,3, 215-224; Pool, J.H., Payne, K., Langbauer Jr., W.R. & Moss, C.J. (1988). The social contexts of some very low frequency calls of African elephants. *Behavioral Ecology and Sociobiology*, 22: 385-392.
12. **Elephant vision:** Kuhrt, H., Bringmann, A., Hartig, W., Wibbelt, G., Peichl, L., & Reichenbach, A. (2017). The retina of Asian and African elephants: comparison of newborn and adult. *Brain, Behavior, and Evolution*, 89, 84-103; Pettigrew, J.D., Bhagwandin, A., Haagensen, M., & Manger, P.R. (2010). Visual acuity and heterogeneities of retinal ganglion cell densities and the tapetum lucidum and the African elephant (Loxodonta africana). *Brain Behav*

Evol, 75, 251-261; visual communication. (n.d.) *Elephantvoices.org* retrieved June 3, 2024 from https://www.elephantvoices.org/elephant-communication/visual-communication.html

13. **Olfactory sensitivity:** Niimura, Y., Matsui, A., Touhara, K. (2014). Extreme expansion of the olfactory receptor gene repertoire in African elephants and evolutionary dynamics of orthologous gene groups in 13 placental mammals. *Genome Research*, 24: 1485-1496.
14. **Working memory in elephants:** Bates, L.A., Sayialel, K.N., Njiraini, N.W., Poole, J.H., Moss, C.J., & Byrne, R.W. (2008). African elephants have expectations about the locations of out-of-sight family members. *Bio. Lett.*, 4, 34-36.
15. Manoochehri, M. (2021). Up to the magical number seven: an evolutionary perspective on the capacity of short term memory. *Heliyon*, 7.
16. **Elephant census:** Chase, M.J., Schlossberg, S., Griffin, C.R., Bouche, P.J., Djene, S.W., Elkan, P.W., Ferreira, S., Grossman, F., Kohi, E.M., Landen, K., Omondi, P., Peltier, A., Selier, S.A., & Sutcliffe, R. (2016). Continent-wide survey reveals massive decline in African savannah elephants. *PeerJ*, Aug31, 4:e2354.
17. Roosevelt in Africa: Lunde, D. (2017). *The Naturalist: Theodore Roosevelt, A Lifetime of Exploration, and the Triumph of American Natural History*. Crown Publishing Group, 247, 253.
18. **Price of a pair of tusks:** Koscak, P. (2023, November 20). Fighting the Ivory Trade. U.S. Customs and Border Protection. https://www.cbp.gov/frontline/fighting-ivory-trade
19. **Critically endangered forest elephant:** International Union for the Conservation of Nature. (2021, March 21). African elephant species now endangered and critically endangered-IUCN red list. [press release]. http://www.Iucn.org/news/species/202103/African-elephant-species-now-endangered-and-critically-endangered-iucn-red-list

CHAPTER 2: RAIN

1. **Seasonality of food choices:** Owen-Smith, N., & Chafota, J. (2012). Selective feeding by a megaherbivore, the African elephant (*Loxodonta africana). Journal of Mammology*, 93(3): 698-705.
2. **Changes in temperature and rainfall:** Climate Change Adaptation in Zambia (February 2012). USAID retrieved February 15, 2024 from https://www.climatelinks.org/sites/default/files/asset/document/zambia_adaptation_fact_sheet_feb2012.pdf; Hamududu, B.H., & Ngoma, H. (2019). Impacts of Climate Change on Water Availability in Zambia: Implications for Irrigation Development. Feed the Future Innovation Lab for Food Security Policy, Michigan State University; Zambia climate change overview. (n.d.) *World Bank*. Retrieved February 4, 2024 from https://climateknowledgeportal.worldbank.org/country/zambia

3. Researchers testing elephant deterrents inspired by: Graham, M.D. & Ochieng, T. (2008). Uptake and performance of farm-based measures for reducing crop raiding by elephants. *Oryx*, 42, 1, 76-82.
4. **Sense storms 150 miles away:** Garstang, M., Davis, R.E., Leggett, K., Frauenfeld, O.W., Greco, S., Zipser, E., Peterson, M. (2014). Response of African Elephants (*Loxodonta africana*) to Seasonal Changes in Rainfall. *Plos One* 9(10): e108736.
5. **Brain structure and processing time:** Hart, B.L. & Hart, L.A. (2007). Evolution of the elephant brain: a paradox between brain size and cognitive behavior. In Kaas, J.H, & Krubitzer, L.A. (Eds.) Evolution of Nervous Systems: A Comprehensive Reference, 3, 491-497; Hart, B.L., Hart, L.A., Pinter-Wollman, N. (2008). Large brains and cognition: where do elephants fit in? *Neuroscience & Biobehavioral Reviews*, 32, 1, 86-98.
6. **Elephant hearing frequencies and harmonics:** Acoustic communication. (n.d.) *Elephantvoices.org* retrieved November 20, 2023 from https://www.elephantvoices.org/elephant-communication/acoustic-communication.html
7. **Ossicle sizes and hearing mechanisms:** O'Connell-Rodwell, C.E., Berezin, J.L., Dharmarajan, A., Ravicz, M.E., Hu, Y., Guan, X., O'Connor, K.N., & Puria, S. (2024). The impact of size on middle-ear sound transmission in elephants, the largest terrestrial mammal. *Plos One*, 19(4); O'Connell-Rodwell, C., Guan, X., Puria, S. (2019). Vibrational Communication in Elephants: A Case for Bone Conduction. In: Hill, P., Lakes-Harlan, R., Mazzoni, V., Narins, P., Virant-Doberlet, M., Wessel, A. (eds) *Biotremology: Studying Vibrational Behavior. Animal Signals and Communication, vol 6.* Springer, Cham; Soltis. J. (2010). Vocal communication in African elephants (Loxodonta Africana). *Zoo Biol.* 29, 192-209.
8. **Foot structure:** O'Connell, C.E. (2007). Keeping an "Ear" to the Ground: seismic communication in elephants. *Physiology*, 22: 287-294; Weissengruber, G.E., Egger, G.F., Hutchinson, R., Greonewald, H.B., Elsasser, L., Famini, D., & Forstenpointner, G. (2006). The structure of the cushions in the feet of African elephants (Loxodonta africana). *J. Anat.*, 209(6), 781-792.
9. **Communication over six miles:** Garstang, M., Larom, D., Raspet, R., & Lindeque, M. (1995). Atmospheric controls on elephant communication. *Journal of Experimental Biology*, 198, 939-951.
10. Ear muscles: O'Connell, C.E. (2007). Keeping an "Ear" to the Ground: seismic communication in elephants. *Physiology*, 22: 287-294.
11. **Onion foot:** Bouley, D.M., Alarcon, C.N., Hildebrandt, T. & O'Connell-Rodwell, C.E. (2007). The distribution, density, and three-dimensional histomorphology of Pacinian corpuscles in the foot of the Asian elephant (Elephas maximus) and their potential role in seismic communication. *J. Anat.*, 211, 428-435; O'Connell, C. (2007). *The Elephant's Secret Sense: The Hidden Life of the Wild Herds of Africa.* Free Press, New York, 185.
12. **Internal map of sensation:** Garstang, M. (2015). *Elephant Sense and Sensibility: Behavior and Cognition.* Elsevier Academic Press, London, 24.

13. **Like a mongoose:** Payne, K. (1998). *Silent Thunder: In the Presence of Elephants*. Penguin Books, New York, 52.
14. **Color vision:** Yokoyama, S., Takenaka, N., Agnew, D.W., & Shoshani, J. (2005). Elephants and human color-blind deuteranopes have identical sets of visual pigments. *Genetics*, 170(1), 335-344.
15. **Interpretation of lion calls:** McComb, A., Shannon, G., Durant, S.M., Sayialel, K., Slotow, R., Poole, A., & Moss, C. (2011). Leadership in elephants: the adaptive value of age. *Proc. R. Soc.*, 278, 3270-3276.
16. **Puddles and other habitat creation:** Mali, F.M.M., Banda, P.K.G., Kusamba, Z.C., Babangenge, G.B., Sebe, J.R.K., Lokasola, A.L. Ewango, C., Tungaluna, G.C.G., Akaibe, D. (2019). Preliminary Data on Amphibian Diversity of the Okapi Wildlife Reserve (RFO) in Democratic Republic of the Congo, *American Journal of Zoology*, 2, 3, 38-43; Nasseri, N., McBrayer, L.D. & Schulte, B.A. (2010). The impact of tree modification by African Elephant (Loxodonta Africana) on herpetofaunal species richness in northern Tanzania. *Afr. J. Ecol.*, 49, 133-140; Pringle, R.M. (2008). Elephants as agents of habitat creation for small vertebrates at the patch scale. *Ecology*, 89 (1), 26-33; Remmers, W., Gameiro, J., Schaberl, I., & Clausnitzer, V. (2016). Elephant (Loxodonta africana) footprints as habitat for aquatic macroinvertebrate communities in Kibale National Park, south-west Uganda. *Afr. J. Ecol*, 55, 342-351.
17. **Drunk elephants:** Morris, S., Humphreys, D., Reynolds, D. (2006). Myth, marula, and elephant: an assessment of voluntary ethanol intoxication of the African elephant (Loxodonta africana) following feeding on the fruit of the marula tree (Sclerocarya birrea). *Physiological and Biochemical Zoology*, 79(2), 363-369; Makopa, T., Modikwe, G., Vrhovsek, U., Lotti, C., Sampaio, J.P., & Zhou, N. (2023). The marula and elephant intoxication myth: assessing the biodiversity of fermenting yeasts associated with marula fruits (Sclerocarya birrea). *FEMS Microbes*, 4, 1-16.
18. **Bulls drinking inspired by:** O'Connell, C. (2015). *Elephant Don: The Politics of a Pachyderm Posse*. University of Chicago Press, Chicago.

CHAPTER 3: NEW LIFE

1. **Birth story inspired by:** Moss, C. (1988). *Elephant Memories: Thirteen Years in the Life of an Elephant Family*. Ivy Books, New York.
2. **Tusklessness:** Campbell-Staton, S.C., Arnold, B.J., Goncalves, D., Granli, P. Poole, J., Long, R.A., & Pringle, R.M. (2021). Ivory poaching and the rapid evolution of tusklessness in African elephants. *Science*, 374 (6566), 483-487; Verny, T.R. (2021, November 3). Tuskless female elephants: Epigenetics for the absolute beginner. trverymd.com https://www.trvernymd.com/blog/tuskless-female-elephants-epigenetics-for-the-absolute-beginner
3. **Trunk muscles:** Longren, L.L., Eigen, L., Shubitidze, A., Lieschnegg, O., Baum, D., Nyakatura, J.A., Hildebrandt, T., & Brecht, M. (2023). Dense reconstruction of elephant trunk musculature. *Current Biology*, 33, 4713-4720.

4. **Larynx more complex than humans:** Herbst, C.T., Svec, J.G., Lohscheller, J., Frey, R., Gumpenberger, M., Stoeger, A.S., & Fitch, W.T. (2013). Complex vibratory patterns in an elephant larynx. *Journal of Experimental Biology, 216,* 4054-4064.
5. **Elephant vocalizations and communication:** *National Geographic.* (2023, April 30). How elephant families communicate and bond: Secrets of the elephants [Video]. YouTube. Retrieved from http://youtube.com/watc?v=WSmlat8BKpU&t=40s June 3, 2024; Poole, J., & Granli, P. (2021). The Elephant Ethogram: a library of African elephant behaviour. *Pachyderm, 62,* 105–111; Soltis, J., Leong, K., & Savage, A. (2005). African elephant vocal communication II: Rumble variation reflects the individual identity and emotional state of callers. *Animal Behavior,* 70 (3), 589-599; Soltis, J., Leighty, K.A., Wesolek, C.M. & Savage, A. (2009). The expression of affect in African elephant (Loxodonta africana) rumble vocalizations. *Journal of Comparative Psychology,* 123 (2), 222-225; Stoeger, A. S., Baotic, A., & Heilman, G. (2021). Vocal creativity in elephant sound production. *Biology,* 10 (750).
6. **Brain growth:** Sikes, S. (1971). *The Natural History of the African Elephant.* Weidenfeld & Nicolson, London.
7. **Social learning:** Plotnik, J.M., & de Waal, F.B.M. (2014). Extraordinary elephant perception. *PNAS,* 111, 14, 5071-5072.
8. **Birth story inspired by:** Moss, C. (1988). *Elephant Memories: Thirteen Years in the Life of an Elephant Family.* Ivy Books, New York.
9. **Grief and death:** Masson, J.M. (1996). *When Elephants Weep: The Emotional Lives of Animals.* Random House, 52.
10. **Poaching and social disruption:** Gobush, K.S., Mutayoba, B.M., & Wasser, S.K. (2008). Long-term impacts of poaching on relatedness, stress physiology, and reproductive output of adult female African elephants. *Conservation Biology,* 22, 6, 1590-1599; Gobush, K., Kerr, B., & Wasser, S. (2009). Genetic relatedness and disrupted social structure in a poached population of African elephants. *Molecular Ecology,* 18, 722-734.
11. Berga, S.L., Daniels, T.L., & Giles, D.E. (1997). Women with functional hypothalamic amenorrhea but not other forms of anovulation display amplified cortisol concentrations. *Fertility and Sterility,* 67, 6, 1024-1030.
12. Goldenberg, S.Z., & Wittemyer, G. (2020). Elephant behavior toward the dead: a review and insights from field observations. *Primates,* 61: 119-128.
13. Mathewson, S. (2015, Sep 29). Elephants check in at the Mfuwe Lodge. Nature World News. natureworldnews.com/articles/17115/20150929/elephants-check-mfuwe-lodge-viedo.htm
14. **Understanding of human speech patterns and scent:** Bates, L.A., Sayialel, K.N., Nijiraini, N.W., Moss, C.J., Poole, J.H., Byrne, RB. (2007). Elephants classify human ethnic groups by odor and garment color. *Current Biology,*

17, 1938-1942; McComb, A., Shannon, G., Sayialel, K., & Moss, C. (2014). Elephants can determine ethnicity, gender, and age from acoustic cues in human voices. *PNAS*, 111, 14, 5433-5438.

15. **Discrimination of human scent:** von Durckheim, K.E.M., Hoffman, L.C., Leslie, A., Hensman, M.C., Hensman, S., Schultz, K., & Lee, S. (2018). African elephants (Loxodonta africana) display remarkable olfactory acuity in human scent matching to sample performance. *Applied Animal Behavior Science*, 200, 123-129.
16. Wickler, W., & Seibt, U. (1997). Aimed object-throwing by a wild African elephant in an interspecific encounter. *Ethology*, 103, 365-368.
17. **Humans using elephant wells:** Kamau, P.N., Sluyter, A. (2018). Challenges of elephant conservation: insights from oral histories of colonialism and landscape in Tsavo, Kenya. *Geographical Review*, 108, 4, 523-544.
18. **Male adolescent family dynamics:** Lee, P.C.,, & Moss, C.J. (2011). Calf development and maternal rearing strategies. In Moss, C.J., Croze, H., & Lee, P.C. (Eds.) *The Amboseli Elephants: A Long-Term Perspective on a Long-Lived Mammal*. University of Chicago Press, 224-237.
19. **Effects of boundaries:** Thompson, K.E., Ford, A., Esteban, G., Poupard, A., Zoon, K., & Pettorelli, N. (2021). Impacts of African savanna elephants (Loxodonta africana) on tall trees and their recovery within a small, fenced reserve in South Africa. *African Journal of Ecology, 60* (3), 357-366.
20. Mathur, M.B., Epel, E., Kind, S., Desai, M., Parks, C.G., Sandler, D.P., & Khazeni, N. (2016). Perceived stress and telomere length: A systematic review, meta-analysis, and methodologic considerations for advancing the field. *Brain Behav Immun*. 54:158-169.
21. Al Aboud, N.M., Tupper, C., & Jialal, I. Genetics, Epigenetic Mechanism. [Updated Aug 1,4 2023]. In: StatPearls [Internet]. Treasure Island (FL): StatPearls Publishing; 2024 Jan-.
22. Lee, P.C., Bussière, L.F., Webber, C.E., Poole, J.H., & Moss, C.J. (2013) Enduring consequences of early experiences: 40 year effects on survival and success among African elephants (Loxodonta africana). *Biol Lett* 9: 20130011.
23. Seeds primed by elephant gut: Campos-Arceiz, A., & Blake, S. (2011) Megagardeners of the forest—the role of elephants in seed dispersal. *Acta Oecologica*, 37, 542-553.
24. Peel, D. (2011, October 3). Lion Anatomy—The Eye. Retrieved June 3, 2024 from https://danielpeel.wordpress.com/tag/eye-of-the-lion/
25. **Long-term effects of culling:** Shannon, G., Slotow, R., Durant, S.M., Sayialel, K.N., Poole, J., Moss, C., & McComb, K. (2013). Effects of social disruption in elephants persist decades after culling. *Frontiers in Zoology*, 10, 62.
26. Zanette, L.Y., Frizzelle, N.R., Clinchy, M., Peel, M.J.S., Keller, C.B., Huebner, S.E. & Packer, C. (2023). Fear of the human "super predator" pervades the South African savanna. *Current Biology*, 33, 1-8.

27. Moore, L. (2009). Beware the elephant in the bush: myths, memory and indigenous traditional knowledge in north-eastern Namibia. *Cultural Geographies*, 16, 329-349.
28. "Tiny" historical demand for ivory within Africa: Somerville, K. (2016). *Ivory: Power and Poaching in Africa*. Hurst Publishers, 83.

CHAPTER 4: GIVE AND TAKE

1. **Stout woman shaping the ground:** Bradley, K. (1966). *The Diary of a District Officer*, 4th ed. St. Martin's Press, New York.
2. **Elephant lifts her head to see close:** Super, S. (1975). Optometric examination of the African elephant Loxodonta africana africana in South West Africa. *Madoqua*, 9, 1, 45-51.
3. **Leg scratching:** Douglas-Hamilton, I., & Douglas-Hamilton. (1975). *Among the Elephants*. Viking Press, New York, 95.
4. **Ice in the dambo:** Nyanga, P.H., Johnsen, F.H., Aune, J.B., & Kalinda, T.H. (2011). Smallholder farmers' perceptions of climate change and conservation agriculture: evidence from Zambia. *Journal of Sustainable Development*, 4(4), 73-85.
5. **Hydroelectric power and droughts:** Ahmed, I. (2022, December 17). Droughts and dams: the troubled future of World Bank funded hydropower in Zambia. phenomenalworld.org retrieved June 3, 2024 from https://phenomenalworld.org/analysis/droughts-and dams/#:~:text=The%20troubled%20future%20of%20World,deep%20vulnerabilities%20in%20the%20system; Sibanda, N. (2024, April 29). As climate change snuffs life out of hydroelectric sources, Zambia feels need to diversify energy mix. Downtoearth.org retrieved June 3, 2024 from httsps://downtoearth.org.in/news/Africa/as-climate-change-snuffs-life-out-of-hydroelectric-sources-zambia-feels-need-to-diversify-energy-mix-95868
6. **Spatio-temporal knowledge**: Tsalyuk, M., Kilian, W., & Reineking, B. (2019). Temporal variation in resource selection of African elephants follows long-term variability in resource availability. *Ecological Monographs*, 89(2).
7. **Spatio-temporal knowledge and importance of large home range:** Kohi, E.M. (2013). The bulldozer herbivore: how animals benefit from elephant modifying an African savanna. [Doctoral thesis, Wageningen University]. Wageningen University and Research eDepot. http://edepot.wur.nl/252972
8. **Mopane distribution and ecology:** Hartnett, D.C., Ott, J.P., Sebes, K., & Dilthogo, M.K. (2012). Coping with herbivory at the juvenile stage: responses to defoliation and stem browsing in the African savanna tree *Colophospermum mopane*. *Journal of Tropical Ecology*, 28, 161-169; Hrabar, H., Hattas, D., & du Toit, J.T. (2009). Differential effects of defoliation by mopane caterpillars and pruning by African elephants on the regrowth of *Colophospermum mopane* foliage. *Journal of Tropical Ecology*, 25, 301-309; Kohi, E.M. (2013). The bulldozer herbivore: how animals benefit from elephant modifying an African

savanna. [Doctoral thesis, Wageningen University]. Wageningen University and Research eDepot. http://edepot.wur.nl/252972; Stevens, N. (2021). What shapes the range edge of a dominant African savanna tree, *Colophospermum mopane*? A demographic approach. Ecology and Evolution, 11, 3726-3736; USDA (2013, October 2). Weed risk assessment for Colophospernum mopane (Kirk ex Benth.) Kirk ex J. Leonard (Fabaceae)-Mopane. Plant Epidemiology and Risk Analysis Laboratory Center for Plant Health Science and Technology.

9. **Elephant rescue inspired by:** TUTA (The untold tales of Africa. (2024, Feb 7). Watch this elephant stunk in the mud get rescued! [Video]. YouTube. Retrieved July 11, 2024 from http://youtube.com/watch?v=XWRTRbacauo
10. **Water delivery inspired by**: Bressa, R. (2017, March 28). The African farmer who brings fresh water to thirsty wild animals. Lifegate.com. Retrieved July 11, 2024 from https://lifegate.com/african-farmer-fresh-water-wild-animals
11. **Desertification from overburning:** Scigliano, E. (2002). *Love, War, and Circuses: That Age-Old Relationship between Elephants and Humans.* Bloomsbury, London, 32.
12. **Buy an elephant a drink:** Parker, I. (2004). *What I Tell You Three Times is True: Conservation, Ivory, History, and Politics.* Librario, Kinloss, UK, 129.
13. **Regeneration of acacias:** Douglas-Hamilton, I. & Douglas-Hamilton, O. (1992). *Battle for the Elephants.* Doubleday, London, 128.

CHAPTER 5: ELEPHANTS AND HUMANS

1. Chiyo, P., & Archie, E., Hollister-Smith, J., Lee, P., Poole, J., Moss, C., & Alberts, S. (2011). Association patterns of African elephants in all-male groups: The role of age and genetic relatedness. *Animal Behaviour* 81(6):1093–99. 81. 10.1016/j.anbehav.2011.02.013.
2. O'Connell-Rodwell, C.E., Wood, J.D., Kinzley, C., Rodwell, T.C., Alarcon, C., Wasser, S.K., & Saplosky, R. (2011). Male African elephants (Loxodonta africana) queue when the stakes are high. *Ethology Ecology & Evolution,* 23: 388-397.
3. Poole, J.H., Lee, P.C., Njiraini, N., & Moss, C.J. (2011). Longevity, competition, and musth: A long-term perspective on male reproductive strategies. In Moss, C.J., Croze, H., & Lee, P.C. (Eds.) *The Amboseli Elephants: A Long-Term Perspective on a Long-Lived Mammal.* University of Chicago Press, 272-286.
4. Slotow, R., van Dyk, A., Poole, J., Page, B., & Klocke, A. (2000). Older bull elephants control young males. *Nature*, 408, 425-426.
5. Evans, K. E. & Harris, S. (2008). Adolescence in male African elephants, Loxodonta africana, and the importance of sociality. *Animal Behaviour, 76,* 779-787.
6. Benedict, F.G. & Lee, R.C. (1936). The heart rate of the elephant. *Proceedings of the American Philosophical Society*, 76,3, 335-341.

7. Myhrvold, C.L., Stone, H.A., & Bou-Zeid, E. (2012). What is the use of elephant hair? *Plos One*, 7(10).
8. Lillywhite, H.B., & Stein, B.R. (1987). Surface sculpturing and water retention of elephant skin. *J. Zool., Lond.*, 211, 727-734.
9. **Hippo and Rhino skin:** Luck, C.P. & Wright, P.G. (1964). Aspects of the anatomy and physiology of the skin of the hippopotamus (*H. amphibius*). *Quarterly Journal of Experimental Physiology and Cognate Medical Sciences*, XLIX, 1, 1-14; Plochocki, J.H., Ruiz, S., Rodriguez-Sosa, J.R., Hall, M.I. (2017). Histological study of white rhinoceros integument. *Plos One* 12(4): e0176327.
10. Smith, C. (2019, November 14). Rare desert elephants survive Namibia's harshest drylands. https://www.awf.org/blog/rare-desert-elephants-survive-namibias-harshest-drylands
11. **Desert elephants walk 100 miles a day:** Leggett, K.E.A. (2006). Home range and seasonal movement of elephants in the Kunene Region, northwestern Namibia. *African Zoology, 41*, 1, 17-36.
12. Morrison, R. (2022, February 8). Do elephants have culture? Londolozi blog. Retrieved from blog.londolozi.com/2022/02/08/do-elephants-have-culture July 11, 2024.
13. Beker, B.M., Cervellera, C., De Vito, A., Musso, C.G. (2018). Human Physiology in Extreme Heat and Cold. *Int. Arch. Clin. Physiol.* 1:001.
14. **Adaptations of grasses:** Western, D. (2020). *We Alone: How Humans Have Conquered the Planet and Can Also Save It.* Yale University Press, 67.
15. Orphan behavior: Goldenberg, S.Z., & Wittemyer, G. (2017). Orphaned female elephant social bonds reflect lack of access to mature adults. *Scientific Reports*, 7, 14408.
16. **Devastating consequences of Neglected Tropical Diseases:** Neglected Tropical Diseases-GLOBAL. (n.d.) World Health Organization. Retrieved November 20, 2023 from https://www.who.int/health-topics/neglected-tropical-diseases#tab=tab_1.
17. **Poverty and wildlife trade:** Hauenstein, S., Kshatriya, M., Blanc, J., Dormann, C.F., & Beale, C.M. (2019). African elephant poaching rates correlate with local poverty, national corruption, and global ivory price. *Nature Communications*, 10, 2242, 1-9.
18. **Climate change and wildlife conflict:** Abrahms. B., Carter, N.H., Clark-Wolf, T.J., Gaynor, K.M., Johansson, E., McInturff, A., Nisi, A.C., Rafiq, K. & West, L. (2023). Climate change as a global amplifier of human-wildlife conflict. *Nature Climate Change*, 13, 224-234; Trinkel, M. (2013). Climate variability, human wildlife conflict and population dynamics of lions *Panthera leo*. *Naturwissenschaften, 100*(4), 345-353.
19. Reduction of wildlife conflict to benefit humans: Packer, C. (2015). *Lions in the Balance: Man-eaters, Manes, and Men with Guns*. University of Chicago Press, 64, 135, 278.

20. Wilson, E.O. (1986). *Biophilia*. Harvard University Press, 25.
21. Matthews, S.R. (2019). *Murder, Witchcraft, and the Killing of Wildlife: Memoirs of a Police Officer in the Heart of Africa*. Pen & Sword Books, 20-21.

CHAPTER 6: MOVING ON

1. **Wound closure:** Douglas-Hamilton, I. & Douglas-Hamilton, O. (1992). *Battle for the Elephants*. Doubleday, London, 101.
2. **Detection of emotional states:** Garstang, M. (2015). *Elephant Sense and Sensibility: Behavior and Cognition*. Elsevier Academic Press, London, 47.
3. **Elephant exports:** US Fish and Wildlife Service (n.d.) 4(d) Rule for African Elephants. Retrieved from https://fws.gov/international-affairs/4d-rule-african-elephants July 11, 2024; *Journal of African Elephants* (2021, September 23). Namibia's live elephant exports: where are they going? Retrieved from https://www.africanelephantjournal.com/namibias-live-elephant-exports-where-are-they-going/ July 11, 2024
4. **Young male leaning on another:** Payne, K. (1998). *Silent Thunder: In the Presence of Elephants*. Penguin Books, New York.
5. **Bull group dynamics:** Allen, C.R.B., Brent, L.J.N., Motsentwa, T, Weiss, M.N. & Croft, D.P. (2020). Importance of old bulls: leaders and followers in collective movements of all-male groups in African savannah elephants (Loxodonta africana). *Scientific Reports*, 10:13996; Allen, C.R.B., Croft, D.P., & Brent, L.J.N. (2021). Reduced older male presence linked to increased rates of aggression to non-conspecific targets in male elephants. *Proc. R. Soc. B*. 288.
6. We Love Animals. (n.d.) Elephant puts litter into trash can. [Video]. Youtube.com Retreived from https://youtube.com/watch?v=mfLOO2y1iZQ July 11, 2024.
7. **Male age of reproduction:** Hollister-Smith, J.A., Poole, J.H., Archie, E.A., Vance, E.A., Georgiadis, N.J., Moss, C.J., & Alberts, S.C., (2007). Age, musth and paternity success in wild male African elephants, Loxodonta africana. *Animal Behavior*, 74, 287-296.
8. **Water availability and elephant movement:** Leggett, K. (2006). Effect of artificial water points on the movement and behaviour of desert-dwelling elephants of north-western Namibia. *Pachyderm, 40*, 26-34.
9. **Vocalization for reproduction:** Leong, K.M., Ortolani, A., Graham, L.H., & Savage, A. (2003). The use of low-frequency vocalizations in African elephant (Loxodonta africana) reproductive strategies. *Hormones and Behavior* 43(4):433–43.
10. **Estrus in elephants:** Lee, P.C., & Moss, C.J. (2011). Female reproductive strategies: individual life histories. In Moss, C.J., Croze, H., & Lee, P.C. (Eds.) *The Amboseli Elephants: A Long-Term Perspective on a Long-Lived Mammal*. University of Chicago Press, 187-20.
11. **Musth:** Poole, J.H., Kasman, L.H., Ramsay, E.C., & Lasley, B.L. (1984). Musth and urinary testosterone concentrations in the African elephant

(Loxodonta africana). *J. Reprod. Fert.*, *70*, 255-260; Rasmussen, L.E., Buss, I.O., Hess, D.L., & Schmidt, M.J. (1984). Testosterone and dihydrotestosterone concentrations in elephant serum and temporal gland secretions. *Biology of Reproduction*, 30, 352-362; Schulte, B.A., & Rasmussen, L.E.L. (1999). Musth, sexual selection, testosterone, and metabolites. In R.E. Johnston, D. Muller-Schwarze, & P.W. Sorensen (Eds.), *Advances in Chemical Signals in Vertebrates* (pp. 383-397). Kluwer Academic.

12. **Sound location:** O'Connell, C. (2007). *The Elephant's Secret Sense: The Hidden Life of the Wild Herds of Africa*. Free Press, New York.
13. **Helping another elephant eat:** Safina, C. (2015). *Beyond Words: What Animals Think and Feel.* Henry Holt & Co, 61.
14. **Elephants asking for help:** Aragon, R. (2020, May 5). Elephant with an old bullet lodged in his head asks humans for help. animalchannel.co https://animalchannel.co/elephant-asks-humans-for-help/; Schelling, A. (2015, September 17). Desperate elephants shot with poison arrows travel to humans for help. https://www.thedodo.com/elephants-travel-huamsn-help-1353631970.html
15. **Inspired by Enkesha at the Sheldrick orphanage in Nairobi:** Dave Sheldrick Wildlife Trust (n.d.) Enkesha's story. Retrieved from https://www.sheldrickwildlifetrust.org/orphans/enkesha July 11, 2024.
16. Fowler, M.E., & Mikota, S.K. (2006). Chemical restraint and general anesthesia, section 1. In (Eds.) Fowler, M.E., & Mikota, S.K., *Biology, Medicine, and Surgery of Elephants*. Blackwell Publishing, 91-110.
17. **Tusk removal description:** Hanes, S. (2017). *White Man's Game: Saving Animals, Rebuilding Eden, and Other Myths of Conservation in Africa.* Henry Holt & Co., 80; Tekweni. (n.d.) Preserving Nature's Heritage: Rangers Retrieve Ivory Tusks from Fallen Elephant Bull. [Video]. Youtube.com Retrieved from https://youtube.com/watch?v=phzsEHdp5RA July 11, 2024.
18. **Behavior in death:** Goldenberg, S.Z., & Wittemyer, G. (2020). Elephant behavior toward the dead: a review and insights from field observations. *Primates*, 61: 119-128.
19. **Carr did not regularly carry a gun on patrol:** Carr, N. (1962). *Return to the Wild: A Story of Two Lions*. Collins, London (in foreword by the Earl of Dalhousie, G.B.E.

CHAPTER 7: ECOLOGY

1. **Fear and reverence:** Moore, L. (2009). Beware the elephant in the bush: myths, memory and indigenous traditional knowledge in north-eastern Namibia. *Cultural Geographies*, 16, 329-349.
2. **Caterpillars and mopane ecology:** Bara, G.T., Sithole, R., & Macheka, L. (2022). The mopane worm (Gonimbrasia belina Westwood): a review of its biology, ecology and utilization in Zimbabwe. *Journal of Insects as Food and Feed*, 8 (8), 82–836; Hrabar, H.D.N.K. (2007). Indirect interactions between

elephants (Loxodonta africana) and mopane caterpillars (Imbrasia belina) through their shared food resource—mopane trees (Colophospermum mopane). [Doctoral Thesis, University of Pretoria]. UPSpace Institutional Repository. http://repository.up.ac.za/bitstream/handle/2263/29289; Hrabar, H., Hattas, D., & du Toit, J.T. (2009). Differential effects of defoliation by mopane caterpillars and pruning by African elephants on the regrowth of Colophospermum mopane foliage. *Journal of Tropical Ecology*, 25, 301-309; Hartnett, D.C., Ott, J.P., Sebes, K., & Dilthogo, M.K. (2012). Coping with herbivory at the juvenile stage: responses to defoliation and stem browsing in the African savanna tree Colophospermum mopane. *Journal of Tropical Ecology*, 28, 161-169; Kohi, E.M. (2013). The bulldozer herbivore: how animals benefit from elephant modifying an African savanna. [Doctoral thesis, Wageningen University]. Wageningen University and Research eDepot. http://edepot.wur.nl/252972

3. **Elephants approach mopane from downwind and mopane defenses:** M. Friend (personal communication, August 7, 2023); African Plant Hunter. January 12, 2019. Plant communication-the strange case of the elephant and the mopane. [Video]. Youtube.com https://www.youtube.com/watch?v=rHTgEysLPKk
4. **Chemical defenses: Also nutrition and role of rainfall:** Makhado, R.A., Potgeiter, M.J., & Luus-Powell, W.J. (2016). Nutritional value of Colophospermum mopane as source of browse and its chemical defences against browse: a review. *Journal of Animal & Plant Sciences*, 26(3), 569-576; Wessels, D.C.J., van der Waal, C., & de Boer, W.F. (2007). Induced defences in Colophsopermum mopane trees. *African Journal of Range and Forage Science*, 24(3), 141-147.
5. Spence, M.D. (1999). *Dispossessing the Wilderness: Indian Removal and the Making of the National Parks*. Oxford University Press.
6. **Conservation works:** Langhammer, P.F., Bull, J.W., Bicknell, J.E., Oakley, J.L., Brown, M.H., Bruford, M.W., Butchart, S.H.M., Carr, J.A., Church, D., Cooney, R., Cutajar, S., Foden, W., Foster, M.N., Gascon, C., Geldmann, J., Genovesi, P., Hoffmann, M., Howard-McCombe, J., Lewis, T., Macfarlane, N.B.W., Melvin, Z.E., Merizalde, R.S., Morehouse, M.G., Pagad, S., Polidoro, B., Sechrest, W., Segelbacher, G., Smith, K.G., Steadman, J., Strongin, K., Williams, J., Woodley, S., Brooks, T.M. (2024). The positive impact of conservation action. *Science*, 384(6694):453-458.
7. **Protection of land by inhabitants:** Asia Indigenous Peoples Pact, Badan Registrasi Wilayah Adat, Cambodian Indigenous Peoples Alliance, Cambodia Indigenous Peoples Organization, Centre for Orang Asli Concerns, Center for Indigenous Peoples' Research and Development, Federation of Community Forestry Users Nepal, Indigenous Media Network, Indigenous Peoples Foundation for Education and Environment, Indigenous Peoples Partnership, Indonesian Institute for Forest and Environment, Inter Mountain

Peoples Education and Culture in Thailand Association, Jaringan Kerja Pemetaan Partisipatif, Land Conflict Watch, Nepal Federation of Indigenous Nationalities, Network of Indigenous Peoples in Thailand, Non-Timber Forest Products - Exchange Programme, Partners of Community Organizations in Sabah Trust, Promotion of Indigenous and Nature Together, Rights and Resources Initiative, and Working Group ICCAs Indonesia. (2022). Reconciling Conservation and Global Biodiversity Goals with Community Land Rights in Asia. Washington, DC: Rights and Resources Initiative; Nepstad, D., Schwartzman, S., Bamberger, B., Santilli, M., Ray, D., Schlesinger, P., Lefebvre, P., Alencar, A., Prinz, E., Fiske, G., & Rolla, A. (2006). Inhibition of Amazon deforestation and fire by parks and indigenous lands. *Conservation Biology, 20*, (1), 65-73; Western, D. (2020). *We Alone: How Humans Have Conquered the Planet and Can Also Save It.* Yale University Press.

8. **Nutrient cycling:** Stanbrook, R.A. (2018). Assessing the nutrient status of elephant dung in Aberdare National Park, Kenya. *Pachyderm*, 59(1), 86-90.
9. **Ecosystem services of elephants:** Asner, G.P., & Levick, S.R. (2012). Lansdcape-scale effects of herbivores on treefall in African savannas. *Ecology Letters, 15*, 11, 1211-1217; Babweteera, F., Savill, P., & Brown, N. (2007). Balanites wilsonia: regeneration with and without elephants. *Biological Conservation, 134*, 40-47; Beaune, D., Bollache, L., Fruth, B., Hohmann, G., & Bretagnolle, F. (2012). Density-dependent effect affecting elephan't seed-dispersed tree recruitment (*Irvingia gabonensis*) in Congo forest. *Pachyderm*, 52, 97-100; Beaune, D., Fruth, B., Bollache, L., Hohmann, G., & Bretagnolle, F. (2013). Doom of the elephant-dependent trees in a Congo tropical forest. *Forest Ecology and Management*, 295, 109-117; Berzaghi, F., Longo, M., Ciais, P., & Blake, S., Bretagnolle, F., Vieira, S., Scaranello, M., Scarascia-Mugnozza, G., Doughty, C.E. (2019). Carbon stocks in central African forests enhanced by elephant disturbance. *Nature Geoscience* 12:725–29; Bunney, K., Bond, W.J., Henley, M. (2017). Seed dispersal kernel of the largest surviving megaherbivore—the African savanna elephant. *Biotropica*, 49(3), 395-401; Chapman, L.J., Chapman, C.A., & Wrangham, R.W. (1992). Balanites wilsonia: elephant dependent dispersal? *Journal of Tropical Ecology*, 8: 275-283; Ferry, N., Dray, S., Fritz, H., Ipavec, A., Widgley, B.J., Charles-Dominique, T., Bourgarel, M., Sebele, L. & Valeix, M. (2021). Long-term high densities of African elephants clear the understorey and promote a new stable savanna woodland community. *Journal of Vegetation Science*; Kohi, E.M., de Boer, W.F., Peel, M.J.S., Slotow, R., van der Waal, C., Heitkonig, I.M.A., Skidmore, A., & Prins, H.H.T. (2011). African elephants (Loxodonta africana) amplify browse heterogeneity in African savanna. *Biotropica*, 43: 711-721; Midgley, J.J., Gallaher, K., & Kruger, L.M. (2012). The role of the elephant (Loxodonta africana) and the tree squirrel (Paraxerus cepapi) in marula (Sclerocarya birrea) seed predation, dispersal and germination. *Journal of Tropical Ecology*, 28(2), 227-231; Owen-Smith, N. & Chafota,

J. (2012). Selective feeding by a megaherbivore, the African elephant (*Loxodonta africana*). *Journal of Mammology*, 93(3), 698-705; Poulsen, J.R., Rosin, C., Meier, A., Mills, E., Nuñez, C.L., Koerner, S.E., Blanchard, E., Callejas, J., Moore, S., & Sowers, M. (2018). Ecological consequences of forest elephant declines for Afrotropical forests. *Conservation Biology*, 32, 3, 559-567; Schrocker, C. (2022). Elephants and aboveground carbon stocks in a South African protected savanna. [Master Thesis, Swedish University of Agricultural Sciences]. Epsilon Archive for Student Projects. http://stud.epsilon.slu.se/18510; Western, D. (1989). The ecological role of elephants in Africa. *Pachyderm, 12*(1), 42-45; Zyambo, P. (2016). Woodland conversion by elephants in Africa: the search for causal factors, processes, mechanisms, and management strategies. *Open Journal of Ecology, 6*, 93-101.

10. **Impala more abundant where elephants are**: Rutina, L.P., Moe, S.R., & Swenson, J.E. (2005). Elephant *Loxodonta africana* driven woodland conversion of shrubland improves dry-season browse availability for impalas *Aepyceros melampus*. *Wildlife Biology*, 11, 3, 207-213.
11. **Change in mosquito range:** Carlson, C.J., Bannon, E., Mendenhall, E., Newfield, T. & Bansal, S. (2023). Rapid range shifts in African *Anopheles* mosquitoes over the last century. *Biol. Lett.* 19: 20220365.
12. **Congolese millions of deaths:** Meredith, M. (2005). *The Fate of Africa: From the Hopes of Freedom to the Heart of Despair.* Public Affairs, 96.
13. **Fewer than 20 university graduates:** Sachs, J.D. (2015). *The Age of Sustainable Development*. Columbia University Press, New York, 136; Democratic Republic of the Congo. (2018, May 21). Encyclopedia.com https://www.encyclopedia.com/places/africa/democratic-republic-congo-political-geography/democratic-congo
14. **Acceptance of violence:** Nzongola-Ntalaja, G. (2004). *From Zaire to the Democratic Republic of the Congo,* 2nd ed. *Current African Issues* No. 28. Uppsala: Nordic Africa Institute.
15. **Transition of power in Zambia:** Meredith, M. (2005). *The Fate of Africa: From the Hopes of Freedom to the Heart of Despair.* Public Affairs.
16. Gaynor, K.M., Fiorella, K.J., Gregory, G.H., Kurz, D.J., Seto, K.L., Withey, L.S., & Brashares, J.S. (2016). War and wildlife: linking armed conflict to conservation. *Front Ecol Environ, 14* (10), 533-542.

CHAPTER 8: A LIFE APART

1. **Lungs attached to the chest wall:** Brown, R.E., Butler, J.P., Godleski, J.J., & Loring, S.H. (1997). The elephant's respiratory system: adaptations to gravitational stress. *Respir Physiol, 109*(2), 177-194.
2. **Risk of injury from not being able to get away from each other:** M. Hartley (personal communication, June 21, 2021)
3. **Male elephants solitary by age four or five:** C. Doyle (personal communication, May 4, 2021); Prado-Oviedo, N.A., Bonaparte-Saller, M.K.,

Malloy, E.J., Meehan, C.L., Mench, J.A., Carlstead, K., & Brown, J.L. (2016). Evaluation of demographics and social life events of Asian (Elephas maximus) and African elephants (Loxodonta africana) in North American zoos. *Plos One* 11 (7): e0154750.

4. **Hormonal vaccines:** Lueders, I., Oerke, A.-K., Knauf-Witzens, T., Young, D. & Bertschinger, H.J. (2019). Use of gonadotropin releasing hormone (GnRH) vaccines for behavioural and reproductive control in managed Asian elephant *Elephas maximus* and African elephant *Loxodonta* africana populations. *Int. Zoo.Yb*. 53, 138-150.
5. **Reducing their feed to keep them malnourished and reducing their water so they stay mildly dehydrated can stop their normal hormonal surges:** E. McWilliam (personal communication, June 13, 2021)
6. Scigliano, E. (2002). *Love, War, and Circuses: That Age-Old Relationship between Elephants and Humans*. Bloomsbury, London, 14.
7. Anthony, L. (2009). *The Elephant Whisperer: My Life with the Herd in the African Wild*. St. Martin's Press, 84-85.
8. Sheldrick, D. (2012). *Love, Life, and Elephants: An African Love Story*. Picador, New York, 290-291.
9. **Bull moving his feet for tortoise:** Payne, K. (1998). *Silent Thunder: In the Presence of Elephants*. Penguin Books, New York, 72.
10. Wilson, E.O. (1986). *Biophilia*. Harvard University Press, 25.
11. Douglas-Hamilton, I. & Douglas-Hamilton, O. (1992). *Battle for the Elephants*. Doubleday, London, 101.
12. Despret, V. (2016). *What Would Animals Say If We Asked the Right Questions?* (B. Buchanan, Trans.). University of Minnesota Press. (Original work published 2012), 170.

CHAPTER 9: FIRE

1. Hoerner, F., Lawrenz, A., Oerke, A., Muller, D.W.H., Azugo-Sepe, I., Roller, M., Damerau, K., & Preisfeld, A. (2023). Long-term olfactory memory in African elephants. *Animals, 13*, 679.
2. **Orphan acceptance inspired by:** David Sheperd wildlife Foundation. (2018, August 6). Elephant orphans adopted by wild herd! Retrieved from https://davidshepherd.org/news-events-insights/news/elephant-orphans-adopted-wild-herd/ July 11, 2024.
3. Elephant knowledge of fire: Anthony, L. (2009). *The Elephant Whisperer: My Life with the Herd in the African Wild*. St. Martin's Press, 179-188.

References

Ache, B.W., Hein, A.M., Bobkov, Y.V., & Principe, J.C. (2016). Smelling time: a neural basis for olfactory scene analysis. *Trends Neurosci.*, 39(10), 649-655.

Attiwill, P.M., Adams, M. A. (1993). Tansley review no. 50 nutrient cycling in forests. *New Phytol. 124*, 561-582.

Bates, L.A., Poole, J.H., & Byrne, R.W. (2008) Elephant cognition. *Current Biology*, 18, 13.

Berry, P.S.M., & Bercovitch, F.B. (2016). Seasonal and geographical influences on the feeding ecology of giraffes in the Luangwa Valley, Zambia 1973-2014. *African Journal of Ecology*, 55, 1, 80-90.

Bradshaw, G.A., & Schore, A.N. (2007). How elephants are opening doors: developmental neuroethology, attachment and social context. *Ethology*, 113, 426-436.

Bradshaw, G.A. (2009). *Elephants on the Edge: What Animals Teach Us about Humanity*. Yale University Press, New Haven.

Byrne, R.W., Bates, L.A., & Moss, C.J. (2009). Elephant cognition in primate perspective. *Comparative Cognition & Behavior Reviews, 4*, 65-79.

Cerling, T.E., Harris, J.M., & Leakey, M.G. (1999). Browsing and grazing in elephants: the isotope record of modern and fossil proboscideans. *Oecologia*, 120, 364-374.

Goldenberg, S.Z., de Silva, S., Rasmussen, H.B., Douglas-Hamilton, I., & Wittemyer, G. (2014). Controlling for behavioural state reveals social dynamics among male African elephants, Loxodonta africana. *Animal Behaviour*, 95, 111-119.

Hartley, M., Wood, A, & Yon, L. (2019). Facilitating the social behaviour of bull elephants in zoos. *Int. Zoo Yb.*, 53: 62-77.

Hildebrandt, T.B., Lueders, I., Hermes, R., Goeritz, F., & Saragusty, J. (2012). Anatomical, physiological, behavioral and pathological aspects of the estrous cycle in elephants. *Jpn. J. Zoo. Wildl. Med.* 17, (3), 97-109.

Holdrege, C. (Spring 2001). Elephantine intelligence. *In Contex*. The Nature Institute (5).

Kinahan, A.A., Pimm, S.L. & van Aarde, R.J. (2007). Ambient temperature as a determinant of landscape use in the savanna elephant, Loxodonta africana. *Journal of Thermal Biology*, 32, 47-58.

Lee, P.C., & Moss, C.J. (2012). Wild female African elephants (Loxodonta africana) exhibit personality traits of leadership and social integration. *Journal of Comparative Psychology*, *123* (3), 224-232.

McArthur, C., Finnerty, P.B., Schmitt, M.H., Shuttleworth, A., & Shrader, A.M. (2019). Plant volatiles are a salient cue for foraging mammals: elephants target preferred plants despite background plant odour. *Animal Behavior*, 155, 199-216.

Ngene, S., Okello, M.M., Mukeka, J., Muya, S., Njumbi, S., Isiche, J. (2017). Home range sizes and space use of African elephants (*Loxodonta africana*) in the southern Kenya and northern Tanzania borderland landscape. *International Journal of Biodiversity and Conservation*, 9 (1), 9-26.

Ngoma, H., Lupiya, P., Kabisa, M., & Hartley, F. (2021). Impacts of climate change on agriculture and household welfare in Zambia: an economy-wide analysis. *Climatic Change*, 167, 55.

Osborn, F.V. (2004). The concept of home range in relation to elephants in Africa. *Pachyderm*, 37, 37-44.

Owen-Smith, N., Kerley, G.I.H., Page, B., Slotow, R. & van Aarde, R.J. (2006). A scientific perspective on the management of elephants in the Kruger National Park and elsewhere. *South African Journal of Science*, *102*, 389-394.

Parker, J.M., Webb, C.T., Daballen, D., Goldenberg, S.Z., Lepirei, J., Letitiya, D., Lolchuragi, D., Leadismo, C., Douglas-Hamilton, I., & Wittemyer, G. (2021). Poaching of African elephants indirectly decreases population growth through lowered orphan survival. *Curr Biol.*, 31(18), 4156-4162.

Pinter-Wollman, N., Isbell, L.A., & Hart, L.A. (2009). The relationship between social behavior and habitat familiarity in African elephants (*Loxodonta africana*). *Proceedings of the Royal Society of London*, 276, 1009-1014.

Polansky, L., Kilian, W. & Wittemyer, G. (2015). Elucidating the significance of spatial memory on movement decisions by African savannah elephants using state—space models. *Proc. R. Soc. B*, 282: 20143042.

Romero, L.M. (2004). Physiological stress in ecology: lessons from biomedical research. *Trends in Ecology and Evolution*, 19, 249-255.

Schulte, B.A., & LaDue, C.A. (2021). The chemical ecology of elephants: 21st century additions to our understanding and future outlooks. *Animals*, 11(2860).

Sillero-Zubiri, C., Sukumar, R. & Treves, A. (2007). Living with wildlife: The roots of conflict and the solutions. In: *Key Topics in Conservation Biology*, eds. David Macdonald and Katrina Service.

Stern, R.D., & Cooper, P.J.M. (2011). Assessing climate risk and climate change using rainfall data—a case study from Zambia. *Exlp Agric*. 47(2), 241-266.

Tapiwa, K.A. (2019). Harvesting and utilization of Marula (Sclerocarya birrea) by Smallholder farmers: A review. *JOJ Wildlife and Biodiversity*, *1*(3), 76-79.

Thurlow, J., Zhu, T., & Diao, X. (2011). Current climate variability and future climate change: estimated growth and poverty impacts for Zambia. WIDER Working Paper, No. 2011/85, The United Nations University World Institute for Development Economics Research (UNU-WIDER), Helsinki.

van Aarde, R.J., Jackson, T.P., & Ferreira, S.M. (2006). Conservation science and elephant management in Southern Africa. *South African Journal of Science*, 102, 385-388.

Wall, J., Wittemyer, G., Klinkenberg, B., LeMay, V., & Douglas-Hamilton, I. (2013). Characterizing properties and drivers of long distance movements by elephants (*Loxodonta africana*) in Gourma, Mali. *Biological Conservation*, *157*, 60-68.

Wilkie, R.D., & Douglas-Hamilton, I. (2018). High-resolution tracking technology reveals distinct patterns in nocturnal crop raiding behavior of an African elephant (*Loxodonta africana*) in Amboseli, Kenya. *Pachyderm*, 59, 41-48.

KNOWING WONDER

Cover artwork and interior illustrations: Gareth Hook
Editing: Todd Shimoda
Publishing expertise: Bruce Rutledge, Chin Music Press
Cover and interior design: Steve Connell | *steveconnell.net*
Printer: Friesens Corporation, Altona, Canada
Typeface: Linotype Electra
Paper: 80 lb. Rolland Opaque Smooth FSC White